TERRY DEARY

Terry Deary is one of the world's most successful authors. He has written over 140 books and is best known for his phenomenally successful *Horrible Histories* series. He has won many awards including the Blue Peter Book Awards "Best Book of Knowledge of All Time" twice. *Books for Keeps* magazine voted him "the outstanding children's non-fiction author of the 20th century", and in 2003 he was the most borrowed non-fiction author in British libraries.

For more information about Terry Deary visit his website: www.terry-deary.com

Ann Evans
The Beast

Sandra Glover
Demon's Rock

Malcolm Rose
The Tortured Wood

Paul Stewart
The Curse of Magoria

The Boy Who Haunted Himself

TERRY DEARY

USBORNE

First published in 2004 by Usborne Publishing Ltd., Usborne House, 83-85 Saffron Hill, London EC1N 8RT, England. www.usborne.com

A CIP catalogue record for this book is available from the British Library.

ISBN 0 7460 6036 X   Printed in Great Britain.

Chapter One

The boy looked at the shabby green door, then back to the crumpled scrap of newspaper in his hand. A chilly gust of wind almost tugged it from his grasp, as he stepped from the shelter of the doorway to examine it in the last of the weak October daylight.

UNLEASH THE SECRET FORCES OF YOUR MIND, said the bold black letters at the top of the advert.

Underneath, in smaller print, it went on:

Improve your memory and amaze your friends!
Develop your willpower and become a success!!

Increase your confidence and impress
the people who matter!!!
Release the hidden power of your
mind through hypnosis.
Consult Doctor Black, 37b Market Street,
Durham City.

The boy strained his eyes to read the tiny print at the bottom...

Special rates for scientific subjects.

He thrust the paper into his pocket, then turned to look again at the green door. There was no number on it but it stood between a grimy greengrocer's shop numbered 35 and an even grubbier newsagent's numbered 39. He glanced at the dusty cabbages to his left. This wasn't how he'd imagined Doctor Black's surgery would be. He'd imagined a fine oak door with a gleaming brass plate.

The dingy, ordinary door gave him the courage to go ahead. He raised a hand to knock on it and felt a sudden fear. It was as if an icicle had been pressed to the back of his neck. Or as if cold eyes were watching him.

He swung round. The people in the street were

hurrying home from the shops, but no one was taking any notice of him. He raised his eyes to the dark windows of the rooms above the shop fronts. If someone was watching from there, then they were well hidden. He shook his head, turned back to the door and rapped boldly on it.

He pulled up the collar of his blazer against the cold of the swirling wind and waited, head bent forward, listening for footsteps behind the door. There was no reply to his knock. He turned the handle gently and was surprised when the door swung open.

The door led onto a stairway. It was dimly lit by a weak, unshaded bulb. The stairs were covered by a worn, red carpet and they led up to a landing with three doors at the top. As he began to climb he noticed a musty smell – a mixture of stale tobacco and old leather, he thought. He guessed that flat "b" must be the one in the middle. He knocked.

"Enter!" a voice behind the door boomed.

The boy opened the door and was surprised by the rich warmth of the scene before him. It was very different from the squalid entrance. The room was warmed by a cheerful, crackling log fire and lit by a brass oil lamp that stood on a polished walnut table. In the flickering light he could see that one wall was lined with fine old books. Two high-backed chairs were covered in red velvet.

"Take a seat by the fire," said the voice. It came from deep inside the chair that faced the door.

"Doctor Black?" the boy asked. He was tall for his age but shrank back into his blazer, shoulders rounded with worry and fear. He could see very little of the man, only a plume of white hair rising from a cloud of amber smoke.

"Come in! Come in, my friend!" The doctor rose to his feet, carefully marked his book before placing it on the table and turned to knock his pipe out on the hearth. "Excuse me," he said. "Filthy habit. Don't ever start, my boy."

"No...I...er..." the boy stammered. The doctor was not very tall but his mane of hair made his head look large and powerful like a lion. His bright black eyes seemed to look right through the boy and made him feel small. Behind him he still felt invisible eyes chilling the back of his head.

"Take a seat! Take a seat!" the old man said, stepping forward to grip the boy's hand in a firm and friendly shake. "Oh, but you're cold!" he cried, with real concern. "Come along. Take this seat by the fire."

"Thank you...Doctor Black."

"Ah! So you know my name!" The doctor's fluffy white eyebrows shot up to meet the untidy tangle of his hair. "I don't believe we've met. I'd have remembered. I've a wonderful memory, you know."

"We haven't met. I'm Peter...Peter Stone."

"Hah! That's good!" The old man threw his head back and laughed loudly. "Peter is a name meaning 'rock'. Peter Stone...rock-stone. That's very good. Whoever gave you that name must have had a rare sense of humour."

"I don't think so," Peter said, blushing. "I don't think my father has any sense of humour," he went on miserably.

The doctor sat down and looked at his young visitor seriously. "I'm sorry. Very sorry. I didn't mean to make fun of you. It's not a laughing matter how a young man gets along with his father. I remember my own childhood..." The old man's voice tailed off and he stared into the crackling flames. Suddenly, he roused himself. "But that was another time, another place. What matters is today...this evening...this very moment. You come all this way to see me and I poke fun at your name. Can you forgive me?" he asked sincerely.

"Of course," Peter said. "Anyway, I haven't come too far. I was on my way home from school." He reached into the pocket of his blazer and pulled out the tattered scrap of newspaper. "I saw this advert and thought you might be able to help."

"Ah, yes," the doctor said with a smile. "I get a lot of enquiries from people your age. You want to increase your hidden mental powers. Well, you have come to the right man."

"Erm, not exactly…it's my exams at the end of the year—" Peter began.

"Of course! You want to increase your memory and amaze your friends! I myself have the most amazing powers of memory, Paul."

"Peter."

"What's that?"

"Peter. My name's Peter."

"Exactly…*Peter*." For a few seconds, the doctor seemed to shrink – a little like a punctured tyre.

"It's about increasing my confidence. Can you give me confidence? Your advert says you can."

The doctor's eyes sparkled. "Of course, my boy. I'm *confident* I can!" He chuckled at his own joke. "After just one session you'll have the nerve for anything. You could walk a tightrope across Niagara Falls…or ask out that young lady you admire so much!" he added, his black eyes twinkling.

"What?" Peter exclaimed.

"Oh, I understand. I was young myself once."

"It's not that at all!" the boy said earnestly. "It's really not. My father says I need confidence to get through these exams, but he can't tell me how to get that confidence. But your advert says you can. Through hypnosis, it says. Can you?"

The old man picked up his pipe and scraped the inside of the bowl with an old penknife. "I could, if I wanted to," he said seriously.

"Please," Peter said. "Please hypnotize me!"

And the ice needles were suddenly sharp at the back of the boy's neck. Sharper than ever. It was as if a secret watcher were waiting for the doctor's reply too.

Chapter Two

Peter Stone's school was four kilometres away from the hypnotist's room. The harsh neon lights blazed over the damp school yard. The tarmac was deserted and the only movement was the swirl of dead leaves and empty sweet packets.

Behind the wide windows, the cleaners moved wearily from room to room. But in one room a girl sat at a desk and stared moodily at a book. She had wide, brown eyes and dark, shoulder-length hair. Her face would have been pretty if it hadn't been for the sulky expression.

The teacher at the desk was broad-shouldered and powerful. He must have been nearly sixty years old with iron-grey hair cropped close to his scalp and cold blue eyes that were small and fierce. His red-brown face looked ugly under the blue-white light and his thin lips were set hard.

The girl looked at her watch. "Can I go now, Mr. Stone?" she asked.

The teacher looked up. "You can go when you have apologized."

"You can't keep me in for more than twenty minutes. Not without giving my mother twenty-four hours' notice," she said.

"You have been here only fifteen minutes, Marie," he told her. He rose to his feet and moved to the door. "If we are not going to get an apology, then we will have to have a formal detention. I'll get the form from the office."

As he closed the door behind him, a shadow moved from the darkness by the waste bins outside the boiler house. A boy strode across the yard towards the classroom. He was tall and broad for his age, but a lot of his size was fat. His greasy hair was pushed back from his forehead and fell to the collar of his leather jacket. Under the jacket was a faded school blazer with the badge hanging by a few threads. He rapped on the window, then pushed his face against it.

The girl jumped and gave a small cry. "Andy!" she mouthed, unsure how close the teacher was.

"Hurry up," the boy said.

"I'm in detention!" she said.

"Silly cow," the boy muttered. Then he pressed his face close to the window again. "You're supposed to be meeting me tonight."

"I know."

"I'll be in the coffee shop at half five. Meet me there," he said.

Marie nodded. The classroom door swung open and Mr. Stone strode in. He followed her gaze across to the window and the pale, spotted face of the boy vanished into the darkness of the yard. "Andrew King," he said sourly. "What does he want?"

"Nothing," the girl muttered sullenly. It was none of the teacher's business.

Mr. Stone walked up to her desk, placed the yellow form in front of her and put his hands on either side of it. He leaned forward, his small eyes bulging a little. "You need a lesson in manners, Miss Allen," he said. "For a start, when you speak to me, you end the sentence with the word 'Sir' or the word 'Mr. Stone'."

"That's two words," she said, looking up to meet his gaze.

He pulled his lips back and breathed deeply through his mouth. "Apologize for what you said in my class earlier today."

"No," she said. "You shouldn't have been picking on my friend Sharon."

"I do not pick on people I..." He stopped himself. "I do not have to justify my class control to the likes of you. No one misbehaves in my lessons. No one says what you said."

"But I did say it," she said calmly.

"And you will have one hour's detention tomorrow night. I will make sure your form teacher is notified and that your class knows what happens to someone as insolent as you," he said in a low voice.

Marie Allen tilted her head to one side and looked at him curiously. "Bet you were sorry when they banned the cane, weren't you?" she asked.

"It was the worst thing ever to happen in education," he hissed. "A quick taste of the cane would have sorted out your friend Andrew King," he breathed.

"And me?" she asked. "Would you have used it to sort me out too?" A pink spot began to appear in each cheek as she slowly rose to her feet, till her eyes were at his level.

The teacher pushed himself back from the desk so he was taller than her again. He snatched the yellow form from the desk and waved it under her nose. "This will have to do instead."

She took the form gently. Keeping her eyes on his she folded the piece of paper carefully and slipped it inside her blazer pocket. "Sorry to disappoint you," she said and, stepping past him, walked into the corridor.

The yard was empty and the security lights at the gate had been smashed at the weekend and not repaired. It was dark in the shadows of the mangy hedge that was planted inside the school fence.

Marie Allen was not easily frightened, but something was making her feel uncomfortable. She stopped and turned suddenly. Mr. Stone was standing at the window of the classroom and watching her cross the yard. She turned and continued through the darkest part, until she was under the protection of the street lights on the road outside.

Suddenly the feeling of being watched grew stronger. She turned sharply again. The classroom was empty and the teacher had gone. She hurried out onto the road and began the walk down into the warm lights of the city centre below.

She didn't look back again. If she had, she would have seen nothing.

Chapter Three

"I will only hypnotize you if I am sure that hypnosis is the answer to your problem," Doctor Black said, and turned to stir the logs into a blaze.

The fire did nothing to thaw the chill Peter felt in his spine. "I need confidence. With confidence I can pass my mock exams at the end of this term."

Doctor Black spread his pale hands wide. "You can get confidence from other people's compliments. Doesn't your father encourage you?"

Peter shook his head miserably. "He tells me

I'm useless. He says I'll never make anything of myself."

"And has he made something of *himself*?" the old man asked. "What does he do?"

"He's a teacher. He teaches Physical Education, and a little English."

"At a local school?"

Peter almost groaned with misery. "At *my* school."

"That can't make it very easy for you," the hypnotist said quietly.

"It wouldn't be so bad if he was just an ordinary teacher..." Peter blurted. Then he stopped. A feeling that he was being disloyal to his father halted him.

"But?" the doctor prompted.

"But...but he's not very popular."

"I see. And I suppose some of his unpopularity rubs off onto you? It must be difficult for you to make friends."

"It is... Oh, it's not his fault really! He was in the army for a long time, you see. He was a sergeant. I think he just got into the habit of shouting at people and making them feel small. He doesn't mean it. He simply doesn't know any other way of treating people. I know he really wants me to do well in the exams."

"So, he tells you that you're useless in the hope you'll try extra hard to prove him wrong. Is that it?"

Peter nodded again. A red spot of anger glowed in the old man's face. He spoke with a sharpness that made Peter jump. "You don't need my hypnotism. You just need one word of encouragement from your father. Just one."

"But he won't," the boy said and felt ashamed as tears pricked at his eyes. "You've got to help me."

"This is a matter for you and your father. I could get you through the exams. But that's not your problem. Your problem is your father. Talk to him."

"I can't. When I try, I clam up. He gets angry, he shouts and I go quiet. We never get anywhere." He reached into his pocket. "I'll pay you. I have twenty-five pounds that I've saved."

Doctor Black waved it away. "My fee is fifty, but I only take on cases where I am sure I can be of some help."

Peter looked at the advert that he'd pulled out with the money. "It says here that you have special rates for scientific subjects. I'd be a scientific subject if you wanted."

The doctor's stern face seemed to melt a touch.

"You would?"

"So long as it didn't hurt," Peter said cautiously.

"Oh, no, no! It's not that sort of experiment. It's a study of the mind under hypnosis. Something I've been studying for almost fifty years. A state called *regression*. Ever heard of it?"

Peter shook his head. The doctor sat in the chair at the far side of the fireplace and filled his pipe. "A human being is made up of a body and a mind," he said. "Some people believe that, when the body dies, the mind dies with it. I believe that the mind lives on."

Peter nodded. "As a ghost?"

"If you like. But I don't believe these ghosts hover in the air or wander in the places where they once lived. I believe they enter a new body and start life again as a new person."

Peter frowned. "So…my mind…has lived before? In another body?"

"Think of your body as a car. It travels the road of life, then breaks down and stops and is left to rot. But your mind is the passenger – it simply gets out, steps into a new car and drives on."

The boy was beginning to understand. "Does it do this many times? I mean, does it ever reach the end of the road?"

"That's what I want to find out with my scientific experiments," Doctor Black said eagerly. "You, Peter Stone, can't remember the last car you journeyed in – you can't remember a past life. You are fastened into Peter Stone's body too tightly. If I can separate your mind from your body for just a little while, I believe you will remember your last life. Maybe even the one before that."

"Under hypnosis?"

"Exactly. I have conducted dozens of experiments into regression, as we call it. Some work, some don't. But each time it works we learn a little more." He added quickly, "And there are no ill effects on the patient, I can assure you. They remember nothing of their past lives when they wake from hypnosis."

Peter nodded slowly. He was fascinated. "What about my confidence?" he asked.

The old man took a wooden taper and lit it at the fire. "I would talk to the present-day Peter Stone first," he promised, as he sucked the flame into the bowl of his pipe. "Then, I would try to talk to whoever you were in a past life – perhaps. It doesn't always work."

"And I'll know nothing about it?" Peter asked.

"Not unless you want to. I will make a recording

of what you say. If you want to listen to it at any time then you are welcome."

The boy frowned and shook his head slowly. "I want to go ahead with it."

The doctor sucked hard on the pipe and looked into the fire. "There is one other thing. Strictly speaking, I ought to have the permission of your parents for this sort of experiment."

"But my father's the whole problem!" Peter cried, dismayed.

"I know! I know. But there are rules against what I am doing. Rules to protect young people, you understand."

"You're a doctor."

The old man turned his eyes away from the boy's and toyed with the glowing tobacco in his pipe. He made a noise that sounded like, "Ah...hmm."

"But you *do* know what you're doing," Peter said slowly.

"I've hypnotized people by the hundred," the man said. He laughed nervously. "Never had any complaints. Do you still wish to proceed?"

Peter hesitated. He didn't want to go home without the confidence he'd come to find. In the quiet room, the loudest sound was the ticking of the old clock on the mantelpiece. And in the silences between the ticks there was a deeper silence. It was as if some invisible presence were waiting for him to decide.

"I want to go ahead with it," Peter said finally. "What do I do?"

Chapter Four

Marie Allen trudged down the hill from the school towards the town centre. Now that she was among the well-lit shops she felt more comfortable. She slowed to look in the windows at the clothes and shoes and the latest CDs. From time to time, she looked over her shoulder. She was sure, now, that there was no one following her.

"But there could have been," she mumbled to her pale reflection in a window. "And what did Andy King do? Did he wait for me? See me safely into town? No. He couldn't be bothered to wait."

It had been exciting, at first, going out with Andy. He was a "leader". He was bigger than the rest of the crowd around him, and they were afraid of him. Afraid of his moods and his threats. He never hit anyone, but he didn't have to, the mob gathered round him like junk metal round a magnet.

When he'd first noticed her, she'd been pleased. Pleased to be closer to the magnet than anyone else and pleased to share his attraction. But lately she'd begun to realize that the magnet really did attract the junk of the school. That made her a bigger, brighter piece of junk than the rest of them – but junk all the same.

She kicked a can along the pavement and walked slowly towards their meeting place in the café at the top of the hill. That was another thing. He always decided where they would go – somewhere where he was surrounded by admiring friends – and they never went where she wanted to go. And he always had money, but never paid for her.

"Do you love him?" her friend Sharon had giggled that morning in Mr. Stone's lesson.

Love him? she thought. I don't even like him. He's overweight and he doesn't smell too good either, she decided.

She turned into an indoor market off the main

square to delay tonight's meeting while she thought about it. Maybe tonight she'd tell him it was over. What was stopping her? Fear. Not fear of Andy King – he was all bluff and he only scared the juniors in the school and some of the weaker teachers.

No, she was scared of being "outside" the gang of friends. After being the centre of their envy for the past month, she knew she could soon become the target of their spite.

Stallholders were pulling down the shutters on their booths and turning off the lights. She wandered back towards the exit. A newsagent's and bookshop stayed open later. Marie pushed open the door and let the warmth of the shop wrap itself around her. She began to read the magazines without really taking in the words.

It was quiet in the main square. She looked through the glass shop doors towards Market Street where the poorer shops stood. For some reason, her eyes were drawn to a warm, amber light that came from a window above a shabby green door. It was almost as if a shadow of a shadow were watching her.

She shuddered and pulled another magazine off the shelf.

Chapter Five

In the warm room, an old man spoke in a low but commanding voice to a boy in a school blazer.

"Sit back in the chair and look at the clock on the wall. It is five minutes to five. Look hard at that minute hand and concentrate on it as it moves. You will not see that minute hand reach the hour. You will be asleep."

Something in Peter's mind urged him to rebel, to stay awake in spite of the old man's attempts. But it didn't seem worth the effort.

"You are tired anyway," the man with the wild

white hair said quietly. "You've had a busy day at school and you need the rest."

That sounded reasonable to Peter and he became almost impatient for the hand to edge its way around the clock.

"Your legs feel as if they are made of lead – they are a great weight pressing into the floor – they are quite numb with heaviness. You can barely feel them at all. Keep looking at the clock, keep listening for the ticking…"

Peter didn't need to be told that. The ticking had become a booming in his head. The silences between the ticks as noiseless as the bottom of the deepest ocean.

"Now your eyelids have the same leaden feeling. They are being dragged down, slowly, until they close." Gradually the boy's view of the room faded – the glowing fire and the doctor's pale face blurred. "It is time for you to sleep. Sleep until I tell you to wake. While you are asleep you will hear nothing but my voice and you will obey."

Peter's mouth fell open slightly and he breathed like a sleeper. The man rose from his chair, lifted the boy's wrist, nodded with satisfaction and then let it fall back limply. The doctor's voice became brisk as he instructed Peter. "Confidence, my boy. You have it. Confidence is overflowing. When I wake you, then you will be able to face the world – face your father – with no fear. What will you say to him?"

"Duzzen marrer," the boy mumbled like a drunkard.

"Doesn't matter? What doesn't matter?"

"Nothing! Nothing matters." The sleeping boy's voice sharpened. His eyes opened, but they were looking at a point somewhere behind the clock. "Look, Dad. I know you want me to do well in these exams, but I think I'll do better if you stop leaning on me so hard." He turned his head as if to catch a reply from his invisible father. "You tell me I have no confidence? Well, I would if you had a little more confidence in me." He raised a hand. "That's all right. No need to apologize, Dad. I understand. You worry for me. Well, you needn't worry any more. I'm *confident* I'll do well – do well enough for you to be proud of me."

His eyes closed again and his head sank forward, as if he were tired after lecturing his father. The hypnotist licked his dry lips and smiled. "Good, good, that will do. Just remember, Peter, when you are in a difficult situation, you just repeat these four words to yourself: 'I can do it'."

"I can do it," Peter drawled.

"You will remember nothing of what I've said to

you. But, somewhere at the back of your mind, those words will stay until you need them." By now, Doctor Black had stoked up his pipe until it was hidden by a dense golden fog. He walked over to a walnut table, where he slid open a drawer to reveal a tape recorder. He took only the microphone from the drawer and placed it on the table. Then he pressed the record button.

"Peter?"

"Uh?" The boy turned his head towards the man's voice but his eyes remained closed.

"We talked about exploring earlier memories – even memories of previous lives. Let's start by taking you back to your sixth birthday, shall we? You are six years old today, do you understand?"

Peter's eyes opened and his thumb crept to the corner of his mouth where he began to chew it. His voice, when he spoke, was high and lisping. "I'm thick-th."

"Where do you live, Peter?"

"Bwannen."

"Brandon, is that? And do you live there with your Mum and Dad?" the doctor asked in a gentle, coaxing voice.

"No Mam," came the reply with a vigorous shake of the head.

"Oh...I thought..." the hypnotist stopped. For the first time, he seemed uncertain.

But the child's voice went on. "Mam's gone to live with Granny."

The man thought he might be opening old wounds in the boy's life that might be better left closed. "Never mind," he muttered quickly, "I'm sure she'll be back soon."

But the words just cut deeper into the misery. "Daddy says he doesn't care if she never comes back," the boy said and then quickly sniffed away the threat of tears. The doctor cursed himself for his clumsiness, took a slightly grubby handkerchief from his top pocket and mopped the sweat from his brow. He sometimes felt guilty about spying into the past of defenceless clients like this. But, if he got some good regression tapes, he could finally write that book and make his name.

He cleared his throat and said, "Your name is Peter Stone. But let's go back into the past. A time before this body was even born. Your name hasn't always been Peter Stone, has it?"

There was a long silence from the boy. If the doctor had been looking closely he'd have seen the figure in the chair give a small shudder, as if the invisible icicle at the back of Peter Stone's neck had been given a push. As if something cold and ruthless had slipped into his brain.

Finally the boy said, "No."

The old man's bird-bright eyes glinted in the firelight. "What is your name?"

"Mah...un," the boy said, as if he were struggling to control a strange tongue.

"Morton? Is that your first name or your surname?"

The face twisted with the effort to speak. "Mar – tin."

"Martin!"

"My name is...Martin Lane," the boy said.

A gust of wind howled in the chimney and blew the logs into a cloud of sparks. The boy coughed and opened his eyes for a moment. There was a faint smile on his lips, but the old man didn't notice.

"What year is it, Martin Lane? Tell me what year it is."

Two creases formed between his eyes in a frown as he replied, "Why...it's the year of our Lord, eighteen hundred and forty, isn't it?"

Chapter Six

Marie Allen put the magazine back into the rack. The shop assistant behind the counter looked at her with suspicion. There had been too much shoplifting lately, especially among children wearing that school blazer.

Marie felt she was being watched by the assistant. But there was something stranger and more uncomfortable in the cold and windswept marketplace. The same feeling she had had in the school grounds. Something, or someone, waiting and watching like an animal after its prey. She didn't want to risk stepping outside until it was time for her to meet Andy at the coffee shop.

Marie picked up another magazine and opened it. Her eyes scanned the page but took nothing in. Her gaze was drawn towards the invisible presence that seemed focused somewhere over Market Street.

"Well, Martin," Doctor Black said. "You can open your eyes now." The boy did so and looked at the doctor with a dull curiosity.

"Where...?" he began.

"Don't worry, Martin. I'll explain everything, all in good time. You are in an unusual situation and I don't want to confuse you by rushing this. Just answer my questions first and then I'll answer yours. Okay?"

"Pardon?"

"I said I'd like to ask you some questions..."

"No! I meant, why did you say 'oh-kay'? What does that mean?"

"Ah! I see. I forgot that you were alive before that phrase became popular. It's just another way of saying 'all right'...all right?"

The boy shook his head, but there was a shrewd look in his eye. "What do you mean, I was 'alive'."

The doctor went on quickly, "I want you to tell me where you live."

The boy hesitated, and looked around.

"Why, close by here, of course. I never left the county in my life. This is where I work. I must be in Inglewilde Hall now...though I've never been in this library before. How did I get here?" Before the doctor could reply the boy sat up suddenly and clutched at his chest in panic and confusion. "I was shot! His Lordship shot me...here, in the chest...I remember the pain...the wound...the blood." He searched desperately for it and seemed to be bewildered when he found himself fingering the badge on a school blazer.

Doctor Black stepped forward quickly and put a comforting hand on the boy's shoulder. "Don't worry. That all happened a long time ago."

"The wound's healed?" the boy asked in disbelief.

"Look, Martin, I'll help you and answer your questions if you'll just answer some of my questions."

"You work for His Lordship?"

"I'm a doctor..."

"And you cured me? Brought me back to life?"

"In a way," Doctor Black nodded unhappily. Things were not going as he'd expected them to.

As it grew used to Martin's character, Peter Stone's body had begun to change. The eyes narrowed and the arms and legs tensed as if ready to spring. "What do you want to know, Doctor?" he asked carefully.

"About you, Martin Lane."

"I work for Lord D'Arlay at Inglewilde Hall."

"Are you a farm worker?"

The boy's hands gripped the arms of the chair in a moment of anger. "Certainly not! I'm a groom in charge of—" He stopped suddenly and his lips closed tightly.

"In charge of what?" Doctor Black urged.

"In charge of the ladies' hunting horses," Martin said finally.

The old man spoke casually. He felt he was close to the heart of the boy's story. "Lord D'Arlay's wife?"

"Yes."

"And Lord D'Arlay's daughters?"

"Mind your own business!" the boy exploded suddenly and jumped to his feet. He was nose to nose with the doctor now.

"Tell me, Martin, why did Lord D'Arlay shoot you?"

"What's it got to do with you?"

"I brought you back to life. I have a right to know about that life," the hypnotist argued, his voice rising as he fought to control his patient.

But the boy was no longer listening to him. Doctor Black realized that Martin was looking past his shoulder at the mantelpiece. "Sit down, Martin!" he said sharply.

But it was too late. The boy had seen his reflection in the mirror above the mantelpiece and slowly brought his hand up to explore the strange features. "My face, Doctor!" he said hoarsely. "What have you done to my face?"

The old man gripped the shocked boy by the shoulders and forced him back into the chair, where he stared silently into the flickering fire. "I'll explain." He spoke quickly and his voice rose in panic. "You have to understand that back in 1840 Lord D'Arlay shot you...he shot you dead."

The boy shuddered and the man cursed himself for his clumsiness. "Dead?"

"What I meant to say was that your body died, but your mind lived on. I believe that you became another person with no memory of Martin. Through the years you have lived in a series of bodies."

The boy looked up sharply. "So what year is it now?"

"We're in the twenty-first century now."

The boy's face was like a mask. "So whose body is this?"

"A boy called Peter Stone."

"And where is Peter Stone's mind while I am in his body?"

"Asleep. I put him into a trance while I released your mind from the depths of his brain."

"Released?"

"Yes. I believe that Martin Lane and Peter Stone are the same person. When Peter awakes he will have no memory of Martin."

"No," the boy said quietly with a steel-hard voice. "I am Martin Lane." He looked carefully at the Doctor. "What do you think will happen to me – to Martin Lane – when Peter Stone wakes from his trance?"

"Well...I suppose... I mean..." the old man stammered.

"You think Martin Lane will cease to exist again, is that it? You claim that you brought me back to life. And I suppose you think you can simply kill me off again, but more cruelly than Lord D'Arlay ever did?"

He pushed himself to his feet and the old man stepped back. It was his turn to sink weakly into his chair, his face as pale as his hair.

"I am sorry, Doctor, but I don't want to die again!" Martin was saying. "You've given me a second chance at life and I am going to take it."

Chapter Seven

The door to the newsagent's shop swung open. Marie looked up and saw a girl in her own school's uniform. "Sharon!" she called.

The thin, dark-haired girl with a sharp face and mean mouth gave a tight smile. "Just come for me mum's paper."

The shop assistant stiffened. Two were always more trouble than one. She knew that a second girl could cause a distraction while the first slipped something into her backpack. She locked the till and stepped over towards the girls to rearrange the magazines.

"What you up to?" Sharon asked. Her voice was thin and reedy. "You're late."

"Had a detention with Stoney."

"What did you do?"

"Called him Stone-age Stone as I left the classroom. I was angry because he picked on you like that."

"Well he is a caveman." Sharon sniffed. "What you doing in town?"

"Meeting Andy up at the coffee shop in ten minutes."

"Lucky you," Sharon said and pulled a disgusted face.

"Jealous?"

"You're joking!"

There was a brief, hostile silence as Sharon picked up an evening paper and turned towards the till.

"Sharon!" Marie said suddenly.

"What?"

Marie looked out onto the deserted square. "Want to walk up to the coffee shop with me?"

"No. Got to get home."

"I'll buy you a coffee."

"And a doughnut?"

"And a doughnut."

"What you scared of?"

"Nothing!"

Sharon's eyes were suspicious. "All right, then. But I'm not sitting with fat Andy."

"Thanks, Sharon. Thanks."

Doctor Black's hands were trembling with fear. "Martin!" he groaned. "You have to let Peter's mind take back his body."

"Why?" the boy asked. He was standing square and strong, looking around the room for the quickest way out. Peter Stone's round-shouldered, shy stoop was gone.

"You could never survive in this day and age. You are a boy of the nineteenth century. Things have changed so much."

"What things?"

The doctor licked his lips nervously. "Well...I doubt you can read. It's essential in this day and age. And...and..." Suddenly the doctor tried a new tack. "You must have known lots of people in 1840. Relatives...friends...perhaps one special girl..."

Martin reacted sharply. "How did you know?"

The old man spread his hands. "There is someone for each of us, Martin. What was her name?"

The boy was silent for a long while before he replied, "Helen."

"Helen," the hypnotist repeated quietly. "Don't you realize that Helen must have been dead for over a hundred years? If you were to step outside this house you'd be totally alone in this world. No friends, no home…no Helen."

The boy lowered his head as if deep in thought, so Doctor Black failed to see the slight smile on his face. "I suppose you're right, Doctor," he said finally.

The doctor closed his eyes and gave a relieved sigh. "Of course I'm right, Martin. It's only fair to Peter that you let him live his life to the full."

"I didn't get the chance," Martin whispered.

"You lived more in your short life than Peter has in his life. His life has just been school, exams, and a bullying father. He has a long way to go before he learns about life, the way you did."

Martin Lane nodded. "What do I do?"

"Just sit down and close your eyes."

Martin clenched his eyes a little too tightly. The doctor went into his routine to relax a patient, while Martin listened carefully. At last the hypnotist was sure the boy was fast asleep. "Now, I want you to return to the present. Tell me your name."

"Peter. Peter Stone," the boy mumbled.

"Good, good. Now, Peter, I'm going to count to three, then snap my fingers. When you hear the click you will be awake and will remember nothing of what happened since I sent you to sleep. Do you understand?"

The boy nodded drowsily.

"One...two...three!" *Click!*

The boy's eyes flew open. He looked up and smiled at the doctor. "I'm ready."

"Ready?"

"To be put into a trance."

"Oh, but it's all over," the old man said. He was troubled. He looked closely at Peter. There was something about him that seemed odd. Wrong. He couldn't put his finger on it.

"Really? Oh, in that case, I'll be going," the boy told him. He looked around the room at the three doors, uncertain which one to choose. He finally chose one and walked towards it.

"Peter," the doctor called. The boy ignored the call and opened the door. "Peter!" the man repeated.

The boy turned with a look of surprise on his face, which he quickly covered. "Yes? That's me."

"Peter. Do come back and see me. Let me know how it goes – if the treatment is working."

"Of course, Doctor," the boy said with a grin. He walked onto the landing at the head of a flight of red-carpeted stairs. He began to whistle as he walked down them.

"There is something wrong," the doctor muttered as he twisted his pipe between his thin white hands. The fire still glowed, but he felt cold and had a sick knot in his stomach. "Something wrong. His voice. Peter has a Durham accent. Martin had an East Anglian accent. Now, the boy that walked out of the door…" The old man sat down shakily in his chair. He ran a hand through his tangled white hair and sighed. He wound back the tape but it had run out before he'd woken Peter Stone. "It was *Peter* who left this room," the hypnotist whispered. "It *was* Peter. It must have been. Oh, *God*, let it have been!"

The boy reached the bottom of the stairs and puzzled for a few moments over the fastenings on the door. At last it swung open and he stepped carefully outside.

The late-autumn evening was lightened by the eerie orange glow of the street lamps – just enough light for him to examine his reflection in the darkened window of the greengrocer's shop. He seemed quite pleased with what he saw: short, fair hair brushed forward over a high forehead. The eyes were large and, as far as he could tell in this peculiar light, probably pale blue or grey. The ears were a little large, he thought, as he pushed some hair in place to cover the fact. But, overall, it was quite a handsome face.

His clothes were very smart; the jacket was ridiculously short and the necktie very narrow, but the material was finely woven and the shirt smooth against his skin.

The boy stepped off the narrow pavement to get a better look and was startled to hear a rushing sound from behind him. As the rushing grew to a roar, the boy turned fearfully to look along the narrow street.

With a cry he leaped back into the doorway and pressed himself, trembling, into the corner. "Helen!" he screamed. "Helen!"

Chapter Eight

Peter's mind snapped into life quite suddenly. He found himself staring at a red bus that was roaring down the hill away from him. He was pressed into a shop doorway and, for some reason, the sight of it had left him trembling with fear. Why? He couldn't remember. What was he doing here anyway? He couldn't remember.

Where was he? Outside Doctor Black's door. How had he got there? He couldn't remember.

"What was that?" a voice asked, an echo somewhere inside his head.

"What?" Peter asked.

"That thing...what was it?" the voice persisted.

"A bus."

"What's a bus?"

"What do you mean, 'What's a bus?' Everyone knows what a bus is. I know what a bus is so why am I having this conversation inside my head? Whose voice is this?"

Peter tried to turn his head...it wouldn't move. He tried to swivel his eyes but they seemed fixed in his head. He could see through his eyes but he couldn't control them. "Who are you?" Peter asked. Then he realized that his lips hadn't moved. Yet the other person understood.

"I'm Martin Lane," came the reply.

"Where are you?"

"I'm inside your head."

The idea was too outrageous to be true. "And are you controlling my body too?"

"Yes. I'll show you. I'll close your eyes."

Everything went black. The street and the comforting amber lights were swallowed. With no picture to focus on, Peter was adrift in a vacuum. Then the fear struck him. "Don't do that!" he screamed voicelessly.

The eyes flew open. Martin Lane's mind gave a

silent chuckle. "I can see it's going to be easy to control your mind. All I have to do is close your eyes and you're in my power."

"Why would you want to control my body?" Peter asked, bewildered.

"I need your body because mine died scores of years ago. I need your mind because I'm a stranger in this world. I have to have your knowledge and your memory to survive in this alien place. I don't know about things like buses. You'll have to teach me."

"Why should I?" Peter demanded. The arrogance of the stranger's mind in his body was beginning to annoy him.

"Because, if you don't, I'll punish you," came the reply, and it came with a playful flicker of the eyelids.

"But *why* are you doing this to me?" Peter persisted.

"You'll find out soon enough. Help me to get what I want and you'll soon be free of me. The more you cooperate, the sooner you can have your scrawny little body back."

"If you've got such a low opinion of my body, then why don't you go and find another one?" Peter asked. "You can't, can you? Doctor Black said my mind...has lived before. In another body.

You're just another me who lived in the past, aren't you?"

"I'm not. Doctor Black is a fool and a charlatan. He said he doesn't believe these ghosts hover in the air or wander in the places where they lived. Well, he's wrong."

"You're a ghost?"

"I am."

"But why haunt me?"

"I need a body."

"I mean, why *my* body?"

"Because yours is the most...*suitable*. You're about the same age as I was when I died." The stranger's mood was subdued now.

"You were this young?" Peter asked. His anger melted as quickly as it had grown. His naturally sympathetic nature urged him to do something. "I'll try to help," he said. "What do I have to do?"

"I need to find another host body..."

"You're going to leave me?" Peter asked.

"No. Not yet. I need a second body – a girl's body – for Helen."

"Who's Helen?"

"My...my..." Martin struggled to find the word to express what she was to him, but somehow the meaning came across to Peter.

"Your girlfriend?"

"Is that what you would call her? She was a girl...she was my friend...but she was also Lord D'Arlay's daughter. I was just a poor stable lad. I could never have courted her. She was my lady. But, no...girlfriend will do to describe her," Martin replied and the pain and the sadness of his thoughts were carried to Peter without words.

"So you need to find a girl who has a suitable body for Helen, the way mine was for you? Why?"

"Helen was your age when I knew her...and I think she died soon after me. I mean, when I was shot I lost contact with this world for a while, but I think it was only for a short time. And, when I returned to look for her she was gone."

"And you've been searching for her ever since?"

"Yes."

"But what will you do when you've found a body for her?" Peter asked.

"Invite her to enter that body, and when I've found her we'll...we'll be able to leave together," Martin finished quickly.

There was something about the mood of that message that left Peter feeling uneasy. It was as if Martin were trying to hide a darker truth behind the words.

"Where will I find a girl for you?" Peter asked awkwardly.

"How would I know?" Martin replied impatiently. "It's your world – you're supposed to tell *me*."

"Yeah…it's just…I don't have much to do with girls. Too much schoolwork," Peter tried to explain.

"You mean you're too shy? Why not say so?" Martin asked.

"I am a bit shy," Peter said miserably.

"That's fine. Just find me some place where boys meet girls in your world, then leave the rest to me," Martin said confidently.

"The coffee shop would be best," Peter said.

"Where is that?"

"At the top of this street," Peter said. Suddenly he was thrown into a state of giddiness as Martin swung his head around to look towards the top of the street. The picture in front of Peter's mind swept past him, totally beyond his control. He felt dizzy and his mind automatically tried to throw his body back into balance. The urge was so strong that for a moment he was back in charge of his movements.

"Don't do that!" Martin cried, as the conflict made the body lurch dangerously against the newsagent's window. "Don't try to take control. We can't both do it."

"I couldn't help it!" Peter told him.

"Look, if we're going to get anywhere you have to stay perfectly still – you're just a passenger," Martin insisted.

"But it's confusing."

"If you can't control yourself, then I'll have to shut you up," Martin said impatiently.

Suddenly Peter felt a suffocating blanket of numbness covering him. He was forced back down into his trance-like sleep.

Martin Lane took a deep breath and turned to climb the steep, narrow street. He looked nervously over his shoulder as a car droned up the slope towards him. He pressed himself against a wall as the car went past and then moved slowly after it.

If he'd turned again he'd have seen two girls, dressed in blazers like his own, following him.

Chapter Nine

Most of the shop windows were well lit and Martin Lane gazed with wonder at the displays of modern goods. When he reached a television-rental shop, he was so fascinated by the moving pictures that he almost forgot the purpose of his journey.

Though he struggled to read the sign above the door, Martin guessed that he had reached the coffee shop. The neon lights glared harshly and spilled their cold brightness over the pavement. Music from invisible players drifted across the road and jarred in his brain…strange, tuneless music.

There were certainly girls in the long, narrow room. They sat in twos and threes at red tables sipping lukewarm coffees and staring moodily into the dregs. As Martin watched, a couple rose from one table and walked to the counter. The boy gasped, shocked, when he realized that he could see the girls' legs from the ankle to the thigh.

He took a deep breath and pushed open the glass door. The warm fragrance of the coffee wrapped itself around him while the music made his eardrums throb. The boy stared at the groups of girls. Some stared back, annoyed, some giggled. Most ignored him.

He studied the faces carefully, selected the one who looked most like his Helen and walked over to the table where she sat with a friend. "Excuse me, mistress," Martin began courteously.

The girls exploded into fits of giggles and turned away from his confused frown. Martin licked his lips and persisted. "May I join you?"

"I didn't know we was falling apart!" one girl managed to reply, almost doubled up with choking laughter. The boy failed to see the joke.

He looked confused and hurt. "Excuse me, mistresses. I wasn't aware that I had said anything humorous."

"Anything humorous!" the smaller girl with bleached hair mimicked him rudely.

Red spots of anger began to glow in Martin's cheeks. He bowed stiffly. "Pardon me, mistresses," he said before turning, ashamed and furious, towards the nearest table. He sat down, feeling the eyes of everyone in the shop burning into him. While the girls he'd spoken to rose to their feet and helped one another stagger to the door, Martin glared fiercely, returning the stares of the other customers.

He sent a quick mental message to the true owner of the body. "Peter...wake up...I need your help." Peter's mind surfaced from the depths that Martin had driven him down to. He quickly remembered his situation and what he was doing in the coffee shop.

"What can I do?" Peter asked.

"I will select a young lady. You will use your knowledge of ladies of this world to woo her."

"Woo! No wonder you're not having much success if you're using language like that!" Peter said. Martin made no reply. "Did they laugh at you?" Martin remained silent. "They *did*, didn't they?"

"They were foolish and childish."

"Marvellous." Peter groaned. "They were laughing at your words...but at my body. You are

56

making *me* look foolish. I'll have to live with that when you go."

"Then you'd better hurry up and find a girl for me," Martin snapped. "At your age you must have lots of friendgirls."

"Girlfriends, you mean. And, no, I haven't. I've never had the confidence."

"You have now," Martin put in quickly. "Doctor Black gave it to you. He said that all you have to do is repeat to yourself, 'I can do it', and you will be able to."

"I can do it," Peter repeated slowly to himself. It certainly seemed to make him feel a little more confident. "I *can* do it," he said again, trying to believe it. "You'll have to give me back control of my body," he insisted, wondering if he really could do this.

"Don't fail me," Martin urged.

Peter felt Martin slowly slipping into the back of his mind, but watching, always watching.

The boy reached into his pocket and found some money. He looked at the prices and reckoned he could afford a drink and a cheese sandwich. He left his seat and walked to the bar to buy them. The others in the café were all about his own age, some in his own year at his school, though he didn't know their names. He knew that the pupils in his own class – the *top* class – would have been at home doing homework, just as he should have been. He never mixed with the pupils from the other classes, the ones his father called the *lower grades*.

He remembered his father and his spirits sank. He was going to need an excuse for getting home late.

He ordered his food and drink. He took no notice when the door opened and two girls walked in, one quite tall with fine, brown hair and the other thin and pinched with a newspaper stuffed into her blazer pocket. The thin one, Sharon, took money from Marie and stood behind Peter at the bar.

When Peter turned with his glass and plate he saw that Marie was sitting in the seat he'd just left. He almost dropped what he was carrying when the voice in his head suddenly said, "That's her! That's the girl I want. That's her!"

Peter watched the girl. She was a year below him at school. She'd have been pretty if it hadn't been for the expression on her face. She had a slight scowl fixed there. As if everyone else in the world were annoying her. Maybe that's how a young lady like Helen D'Arlay would have looked and maybe that's why Martin had chosen her.

"I can do it," Peter murmured to himself as he

strode to the table. "Oh, hello!" he said brightly. "I see I've found someone to share my table."

Her brown eyes turned on him and looked him up and down, a shade annoyed. "I didn't see a reserved notice on it," she said and began to rise.

"No, no! Sit down. I'll be glad of the company," Peter said firmly. It wasn't quite an order, yet the girl obeyed. "Can I get you a coffee?"

"Sharon's getting mine," she said, nodding towards the thin girl at the bar.

"Ah." Peter nodded. "You go to the same school as me, don't you?"

She looked down at her badge then across at his and said carefully, "Took a bit of working out that one."

He grinned. "But not the same year."

"No, I'm a year below you."

"Probably why we've never had the pleasure of one another's company before," he said smoothly. She turned pink and looked down at the table. You're trying just a little too hard, he said to himself, and was relieved when Sharon brought a coffee to the table.

"Don't let me interrupt," Sharon said with a glint in her eye. "Just going to talk to the lads in the corner," she added and left Peter alone with Marie again.

"I know who *you* are, of course," the girl said suddenly and with a touch of hostility. "You're Peter Stone. Your dad's Stone-age Stone, my English teacher."

It was Peter's turn to feel embarrassed. "Oh, you know him," he muttered.

She gave a forced smile and said, "I've just come from a detention with him. My boyfriend wasn't very happy. He hates him."

That was a double blow for Peter. She already had a boyfriend *and* she knew he was the son of the school's most hated teacher.

To his surprise Marie's eyes softened a little as she said, "It must be rough having a dad like him."

"Yeah," he answered miserably. "Everybody thinks of me as Mr. Stone's son. They never see me as a person in my own right."

"I can understand that," she said. "I'm just Marie Allen – the one and only."

"Pleased to meet you, Marie," Peter said lightly. She grinned at him, showing fine, even teeth. "What's so funny?" he asked.

"You are," she replied. "You're so...different. Different to the serious boy I've seen walking around the school. Different to what Andy says about you."

"Andy? Your boyfriend? Not Andy King!"

"Oh, you know him? He says you're…"

"I can imagine."

"You don't get on with him?" she asked.

"I…don't get on with him. He seems to think that because I'm in the top class and my father's a teacher then I'm a fair target for him and his gang," he told her.

Marie steered him away from the touchy subject. "You're obviously not a swot. I mean, you'd be working tonight if you were."

Peter relaxed and took the opportunity to change the subject. "No. I've been to see a doctor."

Marie flinched. There was nothing worse than talking about someone else's medical problems. "You're ill?"

"No, he wasn't a doctor of medicine. He was a hypnotist," Peter explained.

Suddenly Martin interrupted him. "Get her interested in the doctor's work. Tell her you can hypnotize her too!"

Peter sent a silent "That's what I'm doing!" message to Martin, then reached into a pocket, pulled out the newspaper advert and pushed it across the table towards her.

Marie studied it carefully, reading it with a mixture of amusement and genuine interest. "And does it work?" she asked. "Have you unleashed the forces of your mind?"

"I went to…to develop my memory. To help with my exams, of course," he lied. "I want to get good grades without doing all the boring revision. But it does work," he said. "Would you like me to show you how Doctor Black hypnotized me?"

Peter tried to sound casual, but he sensed that Martin Lane was lurking just below the surface of his mind, listening intensely, waiting for the girl to give the right answer.

Marie tilted her head to one side and her straight, dark hair brushed lightly against her shoulder. "You think you could hypnotize me?" she asked.

"I couldn't if you didn't want me to," Peter said.

"But if I cooperated?"

"Then I might," he replied.

"Go on. Try it," she said.

That was the answer Martin had been waiting for. He watched as Peter repeated the operations that Doctor Black had used on him. Marie's expression of amusement faded into one of deep concentration. To anyone else in the café they looked like any other couple having an intense conversation. But it was not long before the girl's face froze into a trance.

Peter was just about to question the girl when his mind was swallowed by a sudden black fog. "What? Why?" he gasped as he felt himself forced into unconsciousness.

"I'll take over now," Martin Lane said. It was the last thing Peter heard before he returned to the blackness.

"Helen," Martin said in a low whisper. "Helen! I've found a body for you to enter."

A boy in a leather jacket came out of the car park that led from the old marketplace. He stuffed his hands into his pockets and bent his head against the cold.

He turned into Market Street, passed a shabby old green door and the darkened window of a newsagent's shop. He headed up the hill towards the coffee shop and a meeting with Marie Allen.

Chapter Ten

In the coffee shop the boy and the girl spoke quietly, heads close. No one took much notice of them. The girl's face was changing – from a pouting schoolgirl to a slightly arrogant and puzzled young lady. "Martin?" she asked. "Is it you? Really you?"

"Helen? Are you there inside that girl's body?"

"Yes," she replied. "But you look so different."

"That's because I'm in the body of a boy called Peter Stone." He stretched out a hand and gripped hers. "I've been so close to finding you over the years. After all this time I've found a way we can be together again. And we are. It worked. I always knew you were out there. Close to me."

"But we can't stay here. We can't stay in these borrowed bodies. We're just ghosts," she said and there was a coldness about her.

"We can stay in them for as long as it takes. First you have to learn to control your body. It's quite a nice body," he said with a grin. "But not so nice as the one you had when you were alive," he added quickly.

The girl released her hand and touched her fingers lightly to her face, then to her body and finally her knees. "This girl is only half dressed!" she whispered in horror.

"It's the fashion now. We've been dead nearly two hundred years, Helen. Things have changed. They have machines that run without horses and lights that burn without oil. They have moving paintings of living people and their clothes are so soft and comfortable – though the young women don't seem to wear many of them."

"I can't walk around like this!" the girl said angrily.

Martin raised a calming hand. "It's the girl Marie who's walking around like that – and no one seems to take any notice. You'll get used to it. You've had no body at all for such a long time now. This is our chance."

"Chance for what, Martin?"

"To escape. We can't enter the afterlife while there's unfinished business in this life. We've been wandering between this life and the next since we died. It's a miracle that our minds met from time to time. And it's another miracle that I found two bodies for us to enter. Think of them as anchors for our drifting spirits. We needn't lose one another ever again. Don't waste the chance just because the body isn't properly dressed."

"How did you find these bodies, Martin?" the girl asked.

"You know that as ghosts we're not properly part of this world. We can't see anything or touch anything. But we can *sense* people's minds. There was one place where a man calling himself a hypnotist worked. He was emptying peoples' minds and inviting another spirit to enter. He believed he was looking back into past lives. But he wasn't. The people were being filled with ghosts...ghosts like you and me. I waited till he found someone suitable. A boy called Peter. I played along with the bumbling old fool's game, and pretended to be surprised to find myself inhabiting another body, in another time. But I was prepared. I had been waiting a long time for the right moment and I wasn't about to give myself away and be forced back into the spirit world. And now I've got Peter's body, and I used him to empty Marie Allen's mind and let you in."

Helen nodded slowly. "I sensed her troubled spirit. I've been reaching out to her – have you noticed how troubled young people attract us like magnets attract metal?"

"Yes," Martin said. "It's the young and restless who are open to us."

"We're possessing them, Martin," Helen said. "For how long?"

"Until our spirits are free to pass on to the afterlife. I'm chained here because I was murdered. Your father shot me and hid my corpse. He did that to stop us running away together. He killed me, Helen! Just to stop us being together. He was extremely wicked. My body was never properly laid to rest."

Helen turned her face away so he couldn't see the pain the memory brought her. "I know," she said.

"What about you, Helen?" he asked. "You must have died soon after me. Did you?"

"Never mind that now," she said quickly.

"How did you die?"

"It doesn't matter."

"You couldn't go on living without me?"

"Something like that."

He nodded. "If your father had shot you instead of me…" he began.

"What?" she said.

"If your father had shot you…if I'd been left to face life without you…then I'd have wanted to die too. If he'd killed you then he'd have killed both of us."

Helen shuddered. "You don't know what you're saying, Martin."

"I would have wanted to die." Martin turned sharply. "You didn't…didn't kill yourself so you could join me, did you? Did you care for me that much?" the boy urged.

"Martin, that was all in the past. Forget the bitterness…"

"Forget it? How can I do that?"

Helen closed her eyes for a moment. She opened them again and looked at the bewildered face. It wasn't Martin's face, but it was a good face. "You have to *forget* it because we can't *change* it. We need to think of what we're going to do *now*," she told him. She gripped his hand again. This time she felt the loneliness and desperation of Martin's endless searching through years of darkness – through colourless, empty nothingness. Not light, not dark, not warm, not cold, not life, not afterlife. A mind without a body, stumbling around and from time to time touching other lost minds and asking, *Have you come across a girl called Helen D'Arlay?* And always the same answer. *No. She must have passed on to the afterlife.* And Martin had given the voiceless cry, *No! She'd never go without me! She's here. I'll find her if it takes for ever!*

Helen knew what he'd suffered, for she'd suffered the same. When she finally brushed against his mind she'd been filled with joy…and then despair as he was lost in the emptiness again. Time and again they'd met and drifted apart. Martin was right, in a way. Only by taking a human shape could they stay together for even a few moments. But Martin was wrong…wrong to steal the bodies of two innocent people.

Helen looked up at him. "How can we stay together? We can only live a little while in these bodies. It's not right."

"We have to lay my ghost to rest. Find the place where your father…where he…where I was buried. I have to give my remains the right sort of burial. The sort of burial that cuts me free from this earthly life for ever. We can pass on to the afterlife once I've done that."

Helen felt a sadness. What about her? Martin was always so rash. He didn't stop to think. It would be crushing if he went on to the afterlife and left her behind. Somehow, sometime, she would have to tell him. But not now. "After all those years?" Helen said. "Can we still do it?"

"We have to try," he said grimly.

"Can we even survive in this world?" she cried and curious faces turned towards her.

They brought their heads close together again and Martin spoke in a low voice. "We can survive with the help of the two who own these bodies," he said.

"We can contact them?"

"Certainly. Go ahead. Try it."

Helen closed her eyes. Martin could tell from the shifting expressions on her face that Helen was having a lively *mind talk* with Marie. The silence stretched for several minutes. Suddenly her eyes flew open. "She'll help us, Martin."

"Good. Then let's get out of here now."

"No! Wait! There's a problem!"

"After all we've been through to get this far, *nothing* can stand in our way," he said.

At that moment the door to the coffee shop swung open. A heavy boy in a leather jacket entered. His hair was long and greasy and his face seemed frozen in a fixed sneer. When he caught sight of Peter Stone talking to Marie Allen his blotched face turned purple, his fists clenched and his mouth twisted in disgust and anger.

It seemed as if everyone in the shop had turned to stone. No one moved – no one even seemed to breathe – as they waited for the explosion they knew was going to destroy the peace.

Chapter Eleven

"**W**hat's happening?" Martin Lane asked. Helen closed her eyes for a moment and *mind spoke* to the owner of her body. "Marie says it's something called a boyfriend. A violent person by the name of Andy King. She arranged to meet him here at this time."

"Walk out. Leave him here," Martin said.

"We can't," Helen said, tense. "He thinks he has some ownership over Marie. He may try to protect her with force…and he hates your body. He hates the boy called Peter Stone."

Andy King didn't wait for Helen and Martin to finish their argument. He began to walk towards their table. Twenty pairs of eyes followed him across the floor. An ugly scowl crossed his unpleasant features.

Martin spoke quickly. "Tell Marie to meet Peter outside this place at midnight tonight."

Helen nodded and turned to face the menacing figure of Andy King – he was just a little taller than Peter Stone. His thin lips curled back. "What you up to?"

Martin looked at him carefully and decided against starting a fight in a public place. If they fought to the death, the law officers might catch him and hang him. He turned his back on the boy in the leather jacket.

"I'm talking to you, Stone!"

Martin stopped and turned. "I beg your pardon?"

Andy King stuck his thumbs in his belt and moved closer. He poked his spotted face close to Martin's. He breathed the threat into Martin's ear, but the coffee shop was so quiet everyone heard it. "If I ever see you talking to my girl again, I'll tear you apart."

Andy was pleased with the threat. It sounded

like one of the criminals in the TV crime series he loved so much. He was good at threatening. He'd never had the problem of carrying out the threats because no one ever stood up to him. So it came as a shock when Martin reacted a little differently to the others. He laughed. A gentle, mocking laugh.

Martin Lane stepped past his enemy and towards the door. Andy King clenched his fists and was about to follow him out of the door when a voice said, "Leave him, Andy." He turned to see Marie gripping the table tensely.

The boy shrugged one shoulder and muttered, "I'll deal with him tomorrow...when I have more time."

And when he had more friends around him, Marie knew. She sat down. Marie was back in control of her body again but was confused and shaking. She had enough of a problem with Helen inside her head without sorting out a fight between Peter Stone and Andy. Helen looked out briefly through Marie's eyes and asked, "Why do you like a boy like this?"

Marie had no answer. "Good question," she murmured.

Out on the street Martin breathed the cool air

thankfully, after the steam of the coffee shop, though even the outside air wasn't all that fresh. It hadn't the clean smell of fresh hay or the sharp tang of the horses' stables. This air tasted stale and oily. Even the crisp October breeze couldn't clear the streets of the smell of traffic fumes.

It had begun to drizzle. A fine mist that made Martin blink. He wakened Peter. "I have a few hours to spend before I return here. Where can I go?" he demanded.

"Home, I suppose," Peter said tiredly, waking to his nightmare.

"Which way?"

"Down the hill to the square first."

Martin turned – then lurched dangerously into the road as he struggled with Peter for control of the body. "This is too clumsy," Martin said. "You can take us to your home."

With some relief, Peter felt his senses return. "When are you going to give me back my body for good?" he asked.

"Soon," was all Martin would say.

"What happened back there in the coffee shop?" he asked.

"You'll find out tomorrow when you go back to school," Martin replied with a touch of cruel humour.

Peter walked on grimly and asked no more questions. Martin lay quiet while Peter walked to the bus station and then rode to his home in one of the villages that surround the city.

He was always aware of Martin lurking there, as he occasionally gave a start when he saw something unfamiliar to his nineteenth-century mind. But at least he stayed silent, and Peter was grateful for that. He needed all his mind power to solve another problem.

How was he going to deal with his father when he got home?

Chapter Twelve

Mr. Stone's grey hair was cropped close to his round head so his ears looked huge and his eyes were two pebbles of blue glass set in a granite face. The name Stone suited him. His thin, hard lips were always turned down in disapproval when he talked to his pupils, but his greatest contempt was saved for his own son, Peter.

Peter was a great disappointment to him. The boy preferred working at his computer to boxing. But Mr. Stone persisted and Peter had to box three rounds with his father every Sunday morning. "To work up an appetite for your Sunday dinner," he said. But Mr. Stone had been a boxing champion in his army days and the beltings he'd handed out to his son normally destroyed the boy's appetite.

Still, Peter learned steadily and, now that he had grown stronger and taller, he had begun to do better in the gym. So Mr. Stone turned his critical gaze on his son's efforts in the classroom. "You'll get nowhere in the exams," he said. "Too lazy."

As Peter walked in that evening after meeting Doctor Black, his father was waiting. "Mr. Robinson told me you have an hour's homework this evening."

"Yes, Dad," Peter mumbled.

"Well?"

"I went to the computer club," the boy lied. He'd prepared that story to cover for the visit to the hypnotist. He hadn't reckoned on the trip to the coffee shop afterwards.

"Until this time?"

"We went for coffee afterwards."

"To that place in the city centre?" Mr. Stone exploded, his tanned face turning red with anger. "Only yobs go to that place. I don't want you mixing with that sort of scum."

"No, Dad."

"And don't think I'm cooking dinner for you at this time of night."

"No, Dad. I'm going upstairs to do my homework," he said quickly before escaping.

As he climbed the stairs, Martin surfaced suddenly to demand, "Why don't you stand up to him?"

"Shut up," Peter said bitterly.

He completed his homework in less than an hour while Martin lurked just below the surface of his consciousness...watching. Peter went down to the living room in time for the news. That was when Martin began to bombard him with questions.

What's that? How does it work? What does electrical mean?

Peter did his best to answer the stream of questions with silent thought replies. But it became complicated when his father started a conversation too.

"Done your homework?"

"Yes, Dad."

What is that machine they're showing pictures of on the television?

A tank.

"There's some cold meat in the kitchen for your supper."

What is a tank?

"A gun on wheels," Peter said aloud.

"Pardon?" his father asked.

"I'm going to bed," Peter said quickly and stumbled to the door. He ran up the stairs and flung himself on the bed. A cloud of depression was settling over him. As if his father wasn't a big enough problem…now he had Martin to deal with too. The confidence he'd learned from Doctor Black was slipping away.

"What have I done to deserve this?" he wondered as he peeled off his sweater. Perhaps sleep would help him escape. Perhaps, he thought hopefully, he'd wake to find that Martin was just a nightmare.

"What are you doing?" Martin demanded sharply.

"Going to bed," Peter replied wearily.

"You can't."

"Why not?"

"We have to go out later," Martin explained.

"Out? It's half past nine now. Where would you want to go at this time of night?"

"To meet Helen. I agreed to meet her at midnight at the coffee place."

"Oh, no!" Peter groaned. "That means I'll have to get up at half eleven and ride five kilometres into Durham. There won't be any buses at that time."

"Ride!" Martin said eagerly. "You have a horse?"

"I've got a bike."

"A what?"

"Let's not start that again. Never mind what a bike is for the moment. You'll find out. Now, let's get some sleep."

"You can't go to sleep. You may not wake up in time," Martin objected.

"I'll set my alarm for half eleven," Peter promised. Then he added quickly, "And before you ask, an alarm is a clock with a bell that rings at the time you want to get up. All right?"

Martin agreed warily. Peter kicked off his shoes and lay on top of the bed. He snapped off the light and was soon in a deep, exhausted sleep. Martin's dreams mingled with Peter's and startled horses fled from roaring buses while Mistress Helen D'Arlay appeared on television.

Peter and Martin woke together as the alarm clock jangled on the bedside table. Peter reached across to cut off the noise, but Martin struggled to control the body, the hand jerked and swept the clock to the floor where it continued its clattering ring.

"You'll wake up my father!" Peter told Martin.

"How do I stop it?" the nineteenth-century boy asked.

"Give me back my body and I'll do it."

Peter fumbled, hands trembling, to push the button on the top of the clock. The last echoes died and the silence was total. It was only when he let out a long sigh that Peter realized he had been holding his breath. He groped on the floor for his shoes.

The bedroom door seemed to have developed a hundred squeaks he'd never noticed before and the floorboards on the landing groaned under his weight. By the time he reached the back door, five full minutes later, his shirt was beginning to stick to his back with sweat.

The chill wind whipped his light anorak and the damp shirt turned suddenly cold, making him shiver. But at least the rain had stopped. He watched as a half moon slid out from behind ragged clouds, then wheeled his bicycle from the garage and set off on his journey back to the city. Martin watched, fascinated.

He arrived just as the town hall clock began striking twelve. The girl was already there and she hurried out of a dark shop doorway to meet him. "Oh, Peter!" she groaned. "Let's get out of here."

Marie was trembling and he realized it must have taken a lot of nerve for her to walk through the midnight streets to meet him. "Where shall we go?"

he asked, looking around. He stared at the gaping black mouths of the doorways and alleyways.

"Not the city centre," she said quickly. "There are police patrols out. They nearly spotted me twice. I had to hide in an alleyway." She shuddered at the memory. "And a drunk was in there. He scared the life out of me! I tripped over the pedals of my bike when I ran away!" The words were gushing out in a flood of relief – relief at having someone to share her fear with.

"Take her back to your house," Martin ordered suddenly.

"Let's go back to my house...we can talk there. At least it'll be warm."

Marie Allen looked at him uncertainly. "You mean so Helen and Martin can talk, don't you? It's a long way."

"There's nowhere else."

She shrugged, grabbed her bike and wheeled it down the hill. Peter followed. As they passed the shabby green door to Doctor Black's rooms, Peter could see a light glowing behind the red velvet curtains. An idea began to form in his mind, but suddenly the terror and the suffocating blackness returned.

"I don't know what you're planning...but forget

it," Martin warned. "I am stronger than you and you will obey me or you will suffer." Peter had been afraid of his father. But that was nothing compared with the terror of Martin Lane haunting his mind.

Chapter Thirteen

Peter swayed dizzily and clutched at Marie's arm for support. She gripped his hand and looked anxiously into his eyes. When he'd recovered, it seemed natural for them to leave their hands joined. It was a new experience for Peter – a strange experience, but not an unpleasant one.

It wasn't until they reached the top of the hill that climbed steeply from the city that they spoke again. "Do you know what Martin is planning to do?" Marie asked, as they climbed onto their bikes.

"Well…he just wants to find Helen, doesn't he?"

"But he's done that," Marie pointed out. "Why does he have to meet her tonight? Why can't they just go on to the afterlife together now that they've found one another?"

Peter realized that Marie was right. How could he have been so stupid? But, as he began to think about Martin's real plans, Peter felt the other boy take over again, as if he'd been watching…waiting. Martin had not been looking out through Peter's eyes – it made them both dizzy – so he had no idea where he was when he took control. And for a few horrifying moments he didn't believe it. He was balanced astride the two-wheeled machine, hurtling down a hill at a speed far faster than a man could run. Martin decided this was impossible. And, if it was impossible, then he must fall off at any second.

His hands clenched in fear…but those hands were wrapped around the brake levers. When they clenched, the brakes connected sharply. The bike stopped – the body carried on. If balancing on two wheels was impossible to Martin, then what happened next seemed even less likely. He flew. He shot through the air, twisting and somersaulting till he landed heavily on the road.

In all of his years of horse riding, Martin had never fallen on anything as hard as that road. He lay still for several seconds, a mass of pain, and tried to work out if he'd broken any bones...any of Peter's bones.

Apart from painful bruises on his elbows and shoulders, and grazing on one knee, he seemed to be still in one piece.

"Are you all right?" Marie asked, having circled in the deserted road and returned to the boy tangled in his bike.

"Thank you, Miss. I do not need your assistance," Martin said coldly, feeling the shame and foolishness of his position.

"Oh, so Martin's back," Marie said shortly. "Well, Master Martin, if you don't want *my* help then perhaps you'd better ask Peter for his. It's obvious that you can't ride." She turned and cycled away.

Cheeks burning with anger, Martin finally summoned Peter, who awoke to find his body full of stabbing pains. Martin did not explain but ordered Peter to take over riding the bike, before lapsing back into a sulking silence.

Peter rose stiffly, examined the bike, then set off slowly after Marie. They reached the house without any further mishaps.

Getting into the house was even more unnerving than leaving. This time, there were two of them – and twice as much noise. Peter led the way into the living room but decided against switching on the light. Only the distant street lights and the half moon gleamed through the window to light the pale, serious face of Marie. She sat on the sofa, close to Peter, so they could talk in whispers.

The girl's eyes looked huge in the shadows. Peter found it hard to concentrate and his tongue became tangled in his words. Something about those eyes, and her closeness, made him nervous and uneasy. But it was a pleasant sort of uneasiness that he'd never known before.

Then, before he had a chance to sort out his feelings, there was the smothering blackness again as Martin took over.

"Helen," he said briskly.

"No. This is Marie. Just what the hell do you think you are playing at?" she hissed angrily. "You take over Peter's body, you just about kill him on his bike, and you have the nerve to use me as a body for your girlfriend. What are you up to? When are you going to leave us in peace?"

Martin was taken aback. He was not used to

being spoken to like this by a girl. His masters had bullied and ordered him and treated him worse than their hunting dogs, but never a girl – not even Helen D'Arlay of Inglewilde Hall. "Let me talk to Helen," he demanded.

"No," Marie snapped defiantly. "Not until you tell me where all this is leading."

Martin sighed impatiently and in short, hissed sentences he told Marie of his plan to lay his own ghost to rest so he could pass on to the afterlife.

"And what does Helen think of your plan?" Marie asked. She'd decided she liked the arrogant Martin a lot less than the shy Peter. She wasn't the least confused by the fact that they inhabited the same body.

"She approves, of course," he answered.

"No. Not, 'of course'. I'm going to ask her exactly what she thinks." Marie sank into a deep silence. Only a slight movement of her lips betrayed the fact that she was holding a conversation inside her head. She frowned a few times and finally nodded her head. She looked up. "It's not quite as simple as you seem to think, Martin Lane."

"Why not?" the boy asked suspiciously.

"Look…I'll let Helen take over and she can explain better than me."

But before Marie could pass control to Helen there was a click and the room flooded with light. Mr. Stone stood in the doorway, barefoot and in a woollen dressing gown. "What on earth's going on here?" he demanded.

Chapter Fourteen

Mr. Stone's eyes were red with tiredness, but sharp with suspicion. His large frame blocked the doorway menacingly, his muscular body straining at the seams of his striped dressing gown.

Martin quickly awoke Peter, who stammered and blushed till he was fully conscious and understood the situation. "Dad…we were just… talking…"

Mr. Stone read his son's confusion as a sign of guilt. "At this time of night?" he snorted.

Marie jumped to her feet. Angry. Angry at being caught in this embarrassing situation through no fault of her own. Angry with her teacher for his unreasonable and sneering suspicions. "Mr. Stone, it isn't what you think…"

"Really?" he growled. "So you *know* what I think, do you? I catch my son on my sofa after midnight with a girl of your sort. What would *you* think?"

Marie's rage was bubbling now. "Firstly, I would ask if my son had a reasonable explanation. And second, I am *not* that sort of—"

"I know exactly what you are," the man spat. "I know the sort of scum you hang around with – toerags like Andy King," he went on, breathing noisily and advancing on her. "I do not want my son mixing with your sort. Understand?"

"I understand, Mr. Stone. I understand why Peter has such a miserable life when he has a father like you," she raged.

The teacher turned purple and clenched his fists, as if controlling an urge to strike her. "Get out! Get out! I'll see you in school tomorrow," he added threateningly.

She ignored the threat and pushed past him to the door. "Bye, Peter," she said calmly. With a final glare at Mr. Stone, she turned and left.

The man took a single stride and stood in front of his son. With a sudden whipping action, he delivered a stinging blow to the side of the boy's head. Peter reeled backwards into the armchair and raised his arms defensively. But his father's follow-up was verbal. "You filthy little animal. Now we know why you came home late last night – neglecting your studies. And, worse, *lying* to me about it. In future, you will come home with me in the car at four o'clock. You will stay in your room, working, until at least nine. Do you understand?"

Peter felt tears of anger and shame welling up in his eyes. He didn't trust his voice to reply so he just nodded. As Mr. Stone turned away, Martin flashed a message to Peter. "I've told you. You have to learn to stand up to him!"

"I can't," Peter replied.

"If you don't, then I will," Martin told him.

"No! Please!" Peter's panic was so great he almost spoke aloud. "I have to live with him after you've gone," he went on quickly. "Don't make it worse for me!"

"I would be making it easier for you. Don't forget Doctor Black's advice," Martin said before lapsing back into a smouldering silence. He was angry at losing another chance to talk with Helen. He wanted a good violent argument with someone – anyone – to give vent to that anger.

Mr. Stone turned and left the room. Peter sat in silence. "I can't do it," he thought bitterly. His head ached. His elbow and knee stung. Wearily, he dragged himself from the chair and followed his father from the room.

As he threw himself into bed he thought that things could only get better in the light of a new day.

He was wrong, of course.

When Peter dragged himself from his bed he was stiff from the accident and tired from lack of sleep. At breakfast, his father talked as though nothing had happened the night before. The incident was not mentioned and Peter tried to answer his father's questions in his normal tone of voice.

Martin was strangely silent, though Peter felt he was still there…brooding.

The journey to school was completed without any unpleasantness from his father. It was not until he stepped from the car that the first hint of the trouble to come showed itself.

At the corner of the science block, where most of the smokers gathered, Andy King was standing. He was surrounded by an assortment of the most unruly boys in the school. From the way he spoke to them, then looked in Peter's direction, it was clear what his intentions were.

The gang cupped their hands to hide the cigarettes from Mr. Stone as he walked across to the staff room. When he'd disappeared, their eyes swivelled back to where Peter stood, waiting for the main doors to open. He pretended not to notice as he pulled up the collar of his blazer. It was a pitiful protection against the bitter wind and the colder stares.

The gang, moving as one, threw a dozen cigarette butts to the ground and stamped on them before walking steadily, deliberately, towards Peter. Suddenly the door rattled and the caretaker threw it open. Peter entered thankfully and tried not to hurry or look over his shoulder as he walked down the gloomy corridor. The air was warm and stale. Peter's breath came in short, tense gasps. Echoes of heavy, studded boots crackled behind him.

He stopped when he reached the sanctuary of the form room. He turned the handle. The door was locked. Peter stood patiently by the door, still refusing to look over his shoulder at the approaching gang. Without a word, they formed a semicircle round their victim.

Silent apart from their chewing of gum, they stared at him. Peter stared back. He felt a hysterical urge to laugh at their serious and stupid faces. He looked down at the floor. Seeing this as a sign of weakness, Andy King stepped forward, shouldering his way through the semicircle to face Peter.

"You're for it now, Stone. You are *dead*."

Chapter Fifteen

"What's going on here?" a woman's voice asked. Mrs. Smedley, Peter's form tutor. Short, grey hair, not very tall but with an authority in her voice that made the gang melt swiftly down the corridor, like snow on a hotplate. Peter found himself face-to-face with the teacher – almost as uncomfortable as he'd been with the gang.

"Well, Peter, what was all that about?" Mrs. Smedley demanded.

Peter blushed and muttered, "We were just having a talk, Miss."

"They don't look like your sort of friends," she said as she unlocked the door and led the way into the bright classroom. Chalk dust danced in the rays of the sun.

"No, Miss," he said as he went to his desk.

"In fact, you don't seem to have many friends at all."

"No, Miss." Peter was beginning to feel embarrassed as other members of his form drifted into the room and eavesdropped on the conversation.

"If you have any problems with Andrew King, you will let me know, won't you?" she said.

"Teacher's pet," someone murmured viciously behind him. He pretended not to hear.

To add to the humiliation, Martin joined in. He demanded to know why Peter let so many people insult him.

Peter had no answer. But, somewhere under the shy exterior, his anger was rising. After years of living with his father, he'd learned to swallow his pride and suffer indignity in silence. He could hide the pain it caused...but he couldn't hide it from Martin.

The anger simmered during morning assembly. It was the only thing that kept him awake. And in the first lesson, English, the heaters were blasting out hot air and making Peter's eyelids droop sleepily. His body was tired, but his mind was exhausted. He was almost relieved when Martin took over.

Martin was fascinated by the lesson. He'd never been to school before and had always wanted to learn the mysteries of reading and writing. Helen D'Arlay had begun to teach him the alphabet...but death had cut his education short. As he heard the teacher talking about poetry, he felt the old urge to learn. He also felt the loss of never having read poetry before. It seemed to express feelings so much better than his own clumsy words. Feelings he'd had towards Helen.

If only he'd had the same chances as Peter. If only he could live again, in Peter's time...in Peter's body, even for a few years... A deeper and more evil plan began to form in his mind. Then his thoughts were abruptly cut short.

"Read the last verse, Peter," Mr. Price said. With a start, Martin realized that the teacher was looking at him.

Thinking quickly, he roused Peter. "Read the last verse," he said.

Peter's eyes made out the page of poetry and slowly the swirling words came into focus. In a daze, he began to read the title of the poem. "The Song Of Wandering Aengus, by W. B. Yeats."

"No, no, no! I asked you to read the *last* verse, Peter."

"Sorry, Sir," the boy mumbled, found the correct place and began to read.

"Though I am old with wandering
Through hollow lands and hilly lands,
I will find out where she has gone,
And kiss her lips and take her hands;
And walk among long dappled grass,
And pluck till time and times are done
The silver apples of the moon,
The golden apples of the sun."

"Very good," Mr. Price said warmly. He was a good teacher. "So, tell me what it means," he added.

Martin had been listening very carefully while Peter read and again the nineteenth-century boy took over. "It's about a boy..."

"A boy? Why not a man?" Mr. Price tried to ask, but Martin was talking and not listening.

"...a boy who died. His mind left this world...it tried to reach the afterlife but it couldn't. My mind wandered in a world between earth-life and afterlife...not a place yet not nothingness – *the hollow lands* – that's how it was. Hollow. I was seeking a girl I knew in this world. I swore that no matter how long it took – *though I am old with wandering* – I would find her. And once I find her we'll spend eternity together – *till time and times are done*. And in the afterlife we'll share all of time and space. There'll be no limit to our power so long as we have one another. We'll walk as tall as the universe…the suns and the moons will be like gold and silver apples in our hands."

Martin stopped speaking. The class was silent for several seconds. Even Mr. Price was stunned. No one had ever heard Peter Stone say so much at one time. As the babble of surprised voices rose, the teacher found the voice to silence them quickly. "Thank you, Peter. An interesting explanation – I'm not sure how an examiner would regard your *personal* narrative style – but it's interesting. Thank you."

Just as the teacher was about to set homework, the bell rang for morning break. The class began to pack books with great urgency and Mr. Price decided to let them go. It was Martin Lane who followed the class out into the yard. The afterlife he'd just described was attractive. But so was the thought of living on earth in this strange future. He was drawn towards the idea of staying. He decided to remain in control while he looked around the school. If he was going to stay, then he needed to learn quickly about this twenty-first-century world.

The glass and concrete buildings were fascinating. He ventured into places that Peter Stone would never have gone. He was used to the girls with bare legs now. They didn't interest him so much as the huge areas of glass and the cars on the road beyond the gates.

That's why Martin failed to notice the group of boys who were following him.

Chapter Sixteen

Andy King could scarcely believe his luck. He stood and watched as Peter Stone wandered towards the most deserted area of the school – behind the sports' hall. He signalled to half of his gang to sprint round the outside of the hall to cut off his enemy's retreat. Thirty seconds later, they wheeled around a corner and came face-to-face with the teacher's son.

Martin woke from his daydream to find six boys blocking his way. They stared at him silently. "What do you want?" Martin asked. He wasn't afraid of these bullies.

The boys looked at one another, puzzled. Peter Stone's accent was suddenly odd...foreign. Before they could work out what was strange about the boy, they looked past him to where Andy King was approaching.

"You!" he called. Martin swung round and saw Andy flanked by another six boys. "We want *you*."

Martin recognized the boy. He remembered how he'd laughed at the gang leader's threat the evening before. Martin wasn't laughing now. With King surrounded by a dozen boys the threats seemed a little more real. A beating could put Peter's body out of action for a month, Martin knew. He'd helped Lord D'Arlay's gamekeepers beat unfortunate poachers that they caught. A thrashing with sticks was quicker and more satisfying than taking them to court and locking them away for a year. Martin couldn't risk that sort of beating now.

"Go to hell," Martin said calmly. He knew that running would do him no good. He had to face them – so long as he stayed calm he would confuse them.

Andy King's face turned dark with anger. Why wasn't Peter Stone showing any fear? And why had he adopted that curious accent? "Look, Stone, don't think your daddy's going to help you now...he won't," he said and began circling Martin.

Martin felt tense, but refused to show fear by spinning round in dizzying circles to keep his eyes on his tormentor. Instead, he stared straight ahead. "You're going to keep away from Marie," Andy King went on. "You are not going to talk to her. You are not even going to *look* at her. Okay?"

"*Okay* means *all right*, doesn't it?" Martin asked.

For a moment, King was thrown by the odd reply. Then, suspecting that his rival was poking fun at him, he moved in close and grabbed the lapels of his blazer.

Martin saw this as the opening move in a sporting wrestling contest. He sought his opponent's lapels and bent his head forward to check his grip. That downward glance saved him from a broken nose. For Andy King knew nothing of sporting contests. His experience was that the fastest, dirtiest fighter usually won and he'd thrown his head forward in a vicious butting movement. It was aimed at Martin's nose, but Martin's tilting head took the blow on the top of his forehead instead.

Still, the force of the blow was enough to send him reeling, stunned, and he dropped to his knees. His mind almost lost contact with the borrowed body altogether. It certainly loosened his power over Peter, who came awake with a jolt. He became aware of several things at the same time. His head was bursting with pain, his vision was blurred, but through the watering eyes he could see a ring of hostile faces laughing down at him.

Luckily the blow had stunned Andy King a little too and he'd stopped to allow his head to clear. That was all the time Peter needed to jump to his feet.

Peter didn't know quite where he was or what was happening, but his boxing training took over automatically. The gang had threatened before, but never attacked. Now he was forced to fight, Peter did it the way he'd been drilled by his father.

Andy King stepped forward confidently. Peter jabbed out a left fist and struck him just below the left eye. King's face showed more surprise than pain...and then anger. He looked around at his circle of admirers. "He hit me!" he announced.

"Get him, Andy!" one of the circling group cried. The others joined in with advice on how to deal with the unpopular teacher's son. The advice ranged from the mild *Give him a lesson, Andy* to *Kill him, Andy!* But King decided on a more cautious line of attack. He walked to a position just out of range of Peter's fists and looked his opponent fiercely in the eye.

"You've asked for it now, Stone," he growled. Suddenly, he let fly with a horizontal kick – the sort of blow he'd seen in kung-fu films, though he'd never studied the art properly. Peter was on his toes in a correct boxing stance. It looked a little odd against the gorilla movements of the boy in the leather jacket. Peter swayed easily out of the way of the kick and darted forward to land a solid blow in King's ribs.

"Oooof!" went the crowd – feeling the blow almost as if Peter had struck all of their chests at the same time. Andy King felt it most of all. His natural state of simmering anger – anger against anyone who stood in his way – exploded into uncontrolled fury. His forehead hurt, his ribs hurt, his eye hurt. But, worst of all, his *pride* hurt.

He rushed wildly at Peter, scarcely able to see through his tears of frustration. His enemy was just a blurred shape, but that was enough. He aimed a swinging blow at the calm, fair head. He put all of his weight and strength into that punch. If it had connected, it would have put Peter in hospital – and put himself in the same hospital with broken knuckles. Luckily for both of them Peter ducked easily out of the way.

The force of the swing carried Andy right past Peter. Peter stepped lightly to one side and aimed a careful, chopping punch at the side of King's head. It connected with a solid *clunk* of bone on bone.

King sank to his hands and knees – mouth open and a stupid expression on his face. Slowly he rolled onto his back. He clawed at the air trying to haul himself back onto his feet. But all he managed was to throw some weight onto one elbow. He seemed to hang there for several seconds before the elbow gave way and left Andy King in a twisted, senseless heap upon the ground.

The circle went silent. Without a word, they turned and walked away from the lifeless boy in the leather jacket. They were numb, unable to believe what they'd just seen. Only one stopped, turned back and muttered to Peter, "Well done, Stoney. He's been asking for that for a long time." There was a look of respect in the boy's eyes that Peter had never seen directed at him before.

Chapter Seventeen

Peter didn't feel as if he had done well in beating Andy King. He felt depressed and angry.

But he was angry with King. He was angry with the gang who had put their leader on a pedestal then walked away when Peter had knocked him down. Angry with his father whose unpopularity had rubbed off onto him. But, most of all, angry with Martin Lane.

He knew it was something to do with Martin. Everything was to do with Martin, he thought. He walked into a cloakroom, soaked a paper towel in cold water and pressed it onto his forehead. It was quiet in here. During the fight, a bell had rung to signal the end of break. All the pupils had disappeared into their classrooms now.

The cloakroom smelled of disinfectant and cigarette smoke. Peter breathed the stale air and tried to calm his head. It was throbbing from King's blow and from the pounding pressure of his anger.

"Martin?" he called silently.

"Yes?" the other boy replied immediately.

"You've got to leave me alone," Peter said tensely.

"Why?"

"Because, sooner or later, you're going to get me killed."

"I've been killed," Martin replied. "It's not so very terrible. Better than the life you have."

"My life was all right until you came into it. Since last night I've been almost run over by a bus, catapulted off my bike and nearly thrown out of the house by my father. Now you've got me into a fight with a boy who could have put me in hospital. I suppose it was something to do with Marie, was it?"

"You won," Martin retorted sourly.

"No thanks to you," Peter replied angrily. "Why don't you face it, Martin? You just can't cope with life in the twenty-first century. I've helped you to find your Helen – you don't need me any more. Let me have my life – you go on to your afterlife."

Martin was silent for a long while. Peter began to think that he had lost his ghost until Martin said, "I can't."

"Can't? Can't go on to the afterlife? Why not?"

"The spirit of a murder victim can't leave this world completely until his ghost is laid to rest. The fact is, you have to get me to the scene of my death so I can free my ghost. You have to get me to Inglewilde Hall."

"Where's that?"

"Near Northallerton."

"But that must be eighty kilometres away!" Peter gasped. "How do we get there? And, even if we did, who's to say the place will still be the same? They may have pulled down Inglewilde Hall – I've never heard of it," Peter said desperately.

"We have to try," Martin said urgently.

"Why?" Peter said bitterly. He'd had enough of being pushed around.

"You'll help me…even if I have to force you," was the reply.

"You can't do that, Martin," Peter said. "I've worked out you and your power. You could only enter my body when I was in a trance. But every time you're under pressure – fear of a bus, a fall from a bike, or a head butt from Andy King – then you're forced to let go."

"I'll show you," Martin said, dragging down the black blanket of unconsciousness over Peter's mind. But this time Peter concentrated. He resisted, he pushed back with all the strength he could find. It was like an arm-wrestling match between two opponents with perfectly matched strength. They struggled, the contest swayed one way and then the other, but neither could make the decisive push.

"Stop!" Peter said and felt Martin's effort fade at once as if he were exhausted too. "Look, Martin, this is doing neither of us any good. You need my help and my knowledge of the modern world, and I want you to get out of my head. Let's work together. It makes sense. That way we both get what we want quicker. You can solve your problem and I can have my body back."

"What do you want me to do?" Martin asked quietly.

"Keep out of my head while I'm in school. Let me get through the days without you making problems for me."

"I'll do that to help you," Martin promised. "What can you do to help me?"

"I'll arrange to meet Marie again – and Helen. This time it will be in a safe place. We'll come up with a plan and we'll do it together. Right?"

Martin thought this over for a while, then quietly tried to remember the expression he'd heard a few times now. "Kay o," he said. "Kay o!"

Chapter Eighteen

Peter laughed out loud and the tension between the boy and the ghost eased. He was still grinning when he walked out of the cloakroom. He found himself grinning into the face of his head teacher.

"Ah, there you are, Peter. I looked for you in your classroom, but you weren't there," the Head said calmly. Whatever the problem was, he didn't seem too annoyed, and Peter relaxed a little.

"No, Sir. I had a headache. I'm sorry, I should have told Mrs. Edwards..."

"Never mind. Come along to my room, will

you?" The Head turned on his heel and marched off down the corridor.

He was a tall man with thin hair combed across his scalp to cover a shining bald patch. The long, loping stride carried him around the school at great speed…as lots of pupils found to their cost when he appeared silently and suddenly to put a stop to their fooling around. Peter had to stretch his legs to keep pace.

He'd never been in the Head's office before. He'd always been curious to know what it was like inside. Now he had the chance to find out, he took no notice. He was too distracted by the first thing he saw when the door opened. For there, standing in front of the large oak desk in the middle of the room, was his father.

"Now," the Head said briskly. "Tell me about your fight with Andrew King."

Peter saw it was pointless to deny that a fight had taken place. He had to trust to the Head's fairness. He told the truth, simply, accurately and modestly. The Head nodded and, when Peter had finished, his father asked the question Peter had dreaded. "What was the fight about?"

Peter sighed. "Andy seems to think I'm trying to take his girlfriend from him," he said, blushing a little.

"And are you?" the Head asked.

"No!" Peter said quickly.

"But you have spent some time with her," Mr. Stone put in.

"Yes," Peter said abruptly.

There was a brief silence as if the two men were waiting for him to explain. He didn't. He couldn't. They'd never believe him.

"Yes…" the Head said finally. "Young King has gone to the hospital for a checkup. Are *you* all right, Peter?"

"Yes, Sir."

"Now that we've heard your side of the story, I don't think we need to take the matter any further. Clearly King's tale about you beating him with a baseball bat was a wild exaggeration to save his own pride."

"There were witnesses!" Peter gasped.

The Head and Mr. Stone exchanged an amused glance. "We've spoken to one or two of them already, Peter, and they confirm *your* story." The Head wasn't coming down on Peter as heavily as he had expected him to. "Our wish is that there will be no repeat. This girl who was the cause of the fight…?" he said and left a question dangling.

"I have to speak to her just once more…" Peter said carefully.

The Head nodded slowly. Peter took this as a sign to go. As he turned, the Head said, "Of course we can't have people fighting all over the school. If you have any more threats from this King boy, you must let a member of staff know immediately – tell me, or your form tutor, Mrs. Smedley, or your father. We can't have pupils taking the law into their own hands, Peter. Even in self-defence." It was the nearest the Head came to a reprimand. Peter was amazed that he was escaping unpunished. "You may go," the Head finished.

"Yes, Sir," Peter answered quietly and turned again to go. He glanced at his father and caught an odd, unfamiliar expression on his face. As Peter walked past, he heard his father whisper in a hoarse voice, "Well done, lad."

He could hardly believe what he'd heard. For as long as he could remember, he'd been striving to hear those few simple words of praise from his father. He'd slaved over textbooks in class and at home; he had struggled to please his teachers and only won the contempt of his fellow pupils…all just to hear those words.

The words hadn't been uttered. Until now. And Peter was suddenly disappointed. All that Mr. Stone had wanted was for his son to prove himself by beating another boy in a fight.

Peter sat in depressed silence through the remainder of his lesson. He took in very little. He certainly didn't notice the new respect with which his classmates looked at him. The story of the fight had spread quickly.

Martin was keeping his promise of silence so completely that Peter began to think he'd gone away. It now felt strange not to have him there, listening, questioning. Peter was alone again…and lonely.

At lunchtime, he paid little attention to what he was eating in the school dining hall. He took no notice of the girl who placed her tray on his table and sat opposite him. Until she spoke. "Peter?" she said uncertainly.

"Marie!" he exclaimed. He looked around nervously.

"It's okay," she said quickly. "You don't have to worry about Andy any more. He's gone to hospital for an X-ray on his head." She smiled wickedly. "If it's possible to X-ray an empty space."

Peter didn't respond to the joke. "Look, Marie, I'm sorry about that. I didn't mean to fight him. I think Martin started it."

"Don't worry about it," Marie said. "Andy's been

asking for someone to thump him for a long time. If you hadn't done it, then I'd probably have done it myself."

"But I thought you...I mean he's..."

"Going out with me? He is. But just because he takes me to the cinema once in a while doesn't mean I think the sun shines out of his bootlaces," she said firmly. "And I do not find it flattering to have him threatening every boy who looks at me. It's just childish. So forget about Andy. We have more important problems to sort out."

Peter groaned. "I'm bored of sorting out problems." He told her of the meeting with the head teacher and his father. Then he repeated his *mind talk* with Martin. "I promised to help him, you see. I was hoping you'd come along."

Marie shook her head slowly. "You don't know the half of it, do you?"

"What do you mean?"

She leaned forward, as if whispering would help. "Are you alone? I mean, is Martin listening?"

"I don't think so."

Marie frowned and her large eyes were anxious. "Listen carefully, Peter. You are in danger. Terrible, terrible danger."

Chapter Nineteen

Peter was tired and his head ached. Marie too had dark shadows under her eyes but seemed to have more energy than him. "What sort of danger am I in?" he asked.

She pushed food around her dinner tray as she sorted out her thoughts. "I've had a long talk with Helen D'Arlay. She's a bit of a snob – thinks she's better than common people like you and me...but underneath she is a warm-hearted girl. She's really sorry that she's disturbed our lives like this. Ashamed at the way she and Martin are using our bodies."

"So why did they do it?"

"It's Martin. He brought her back..."

"Yes. To help him lay his own ghost to rest."

"That was the plan...originally. But Helen says he's begun to change."

"In what way?"

"He's very bitter about the past. The fact that he was killed so young. He feels that he was cheated of a full life and he wants to make it up somehow."

"He can't do that," Peter said uncomfortably.

"There is *one* way. He can take over your body...and never give it back," she said softly.

"I can fight him."

Marie shook her head quickly. "You can stop him *forcing* his way into your mind now. But if you hand over your body to him *freely* then he'll never let you back in again. Helen says he can be quite ruthless. He will try to lay his ghost to rest in the afterlife. But, if he fails, then he'll stay in this world – in your body – as the next best thing. He'll steal your body, Peter, as sure as any body-snatcher."

Peter wanted to argue, but he knew she was telling the truth. "What can we do?" he asked.

"We can try to help them. We can go to Northallerton and look for Inglewilde Hall," Marie said.

"That's what I've promised I'll do."

"I know. But you need me with you," Marie told him. "You need me to watch out for you. Martin and Helen can guide us to where Martin's body was hidden and see if we can find any remains – anything at all – then take them to the nearest churchyard and bury them there. That's all it will take."

"All!"

Marie closed her eyes for a moment, then looked up at Peter. "It's a day from our lives, Peter, just a day. What's that compared to the hundreds of years they've been searching for one another?"

"*Through hollow lands and hilly lands,*" he murmured.

"What was that?"

"You're right," he admitted.

"Peace for them and peace for us once they've gone," Marie urged.

He laughed softly. "*Peace* isn't what I'll expect from my father if I disappear with you!"

Some of the old hardness returned to Marie's features. "It hasn't been easy for me, you know. My mother caught me sneaking in at one o'clock yesterday morning after your dad threw me out. She threatened to nail my feet to the bed tonight to keep me in."

Peter winced. "Sorry," he said.

She glared at him. "Andy and me will be finished for good when this is over. My mother will probably have me fitted with a ball and chain until my eighteenth birthday and the girls in my class will think I tried to elope with Stone-age Stone's son! You think I'm going to enjoy this?"

"Sorry," he said again.

She jabbed a finger at him. "This is the most stupid thing I have ever done in my life. And it all started because you went to some barmy old hypnotist to help you pass your miserable exams."

Her voice was rising now and pupils at other tables were turning to look at them. "Sorry," Peter said. "The truth is…I asked him to give me more confidence. It wasn't really about exams. Sorry."

"And stop saying that!" she hissed. "It's so-called *Doctor* Black who should be sorry. Once we get back, I'm going to make sure – personally – that he retires for good. He's opened up a right kettle of fish here."

"Can of worms," Peter corrected her.

She slammed a hand on the table and spat, "Sorry, Mr. Smart-Aleck Stone. I forgot, you know *everything*. Can of *worms* then. Now, start using your Smart-Aleck brain to help me."

Peter stared. "How?"

"We'll have to go home after school. Then sneak out. That way they won't start looking for us till tomorrow morning at the earliest."

Peter nodded. "Makes sense."

"Thank you," she breathed. Controlling her temper, she went on, "Then you have to find the time of the last train to Northallerton. We'll be down there to start searching for Inglewilde at first light."

"I'll use the school computer to look for rail times on the Internet," he agreed.

"And we'll need money for the tickets. I've got about thirty pounds saved. I don't want to have to use it all."

"My mother sends me five a week," Peter said. "I don't spend much. I must have nearly a hundred in my room."

"Bring it all," she said.

"Anything else?"

"While you're on the Internet, find out anything you can about Inglewilde Hall. And find out how we can get there. We don't want to draw attention to ourselves by asking for directions when we get to Northallerton," she said. Then she studied his face for a moment. "What's wrong?"

"Do you think we can do it?" he asked.

She looked up to the ceiling. "Didn't that

dummy doctor do anything for you? Didn't he even give you the confidence you asked him for?"

A slow smile spread across Peter's face. "I *can* do it," he said.

Marie Allen tilted her head to one side so her fine hair fell onto her shoulder. "No, Peter. *We* can do it. *We* can do it."

Chapter Twenty

The last train slid smoothly into Northallerton station. Peter and Marie were the only two passengers to get off. They had sleeping bags rolled and tied with straps that they hung from their shoulders. No one got on the train and only the stationmaster stood on the platform to blow his whistle and wave the train out.

He could finish for the night now, he sighed thankfully. But, as he turned, he saw that the boy and the girl were still standing on the platform, uncertain. "Can I see your tickets?" he asked.

"We showed them on the train. They don't usually..." Peter began.

"I am entitled..." the man said. Peter showed him the tickets. "From Durham, eh?"

"Yes."

"Open return, I see."

"Yes, we're not staying," Marie explained helpfully.

The man nodded. Runaways always had one-way tickets.

"We're looking for Inglewilde Hall," Marie said.

The man rubbed his chin and yawned. "Never heard of it," he said. "It's a bit late to be looking for some place you aren't sure about, isn't it?"

"No," Peter said quickly. He took out a map of the area that he'd printed from the school computer and held it out under the pale platform lamps. "We know where it is. We just weren't sure which way to turn when we left the station."

"I've never heard of an Inglewilde Hall," the man said. "But there's an Inglewilde Country Park about five kilometres out of the town on the York road.

"That's it," Marie said.

The stationmaster walked with them to the exit. "Go to the end of the station drive, turn right and walk towards the town centre. You'll see York signposted."

"Thanks," the girl said.

"But you're not going to walk there at this time of night, surely? You can get a taxi from the town centre."

"We'll do that, thanks." Peter nodded. "Goodnight!"

The man waited a few moments as they walked across the shadowy car park, shrugged, then gathered his keys from his belt and turned back towards the gate.

"Do we take a taxi, then?" Peter asked.

Marie shook her head. "No. He'll ask too many questions. He may even report us."

Peter strode by her side. "They'll be out looking for us in the morning," he said.

"I know. And that gives us all night. But if a taxi driver turns us in to the police, they may come for us before Martin and Helen have finished," Marie argued.

Peter shrugged the sleeping bag onto his shoulder. "So we walk," he sighed.

It took them two hours. The road was busy and they cut across the dark fields and along back lanes till they reached a high fence.

Somewhere an animal roared.

"Lions?" Peter murmured.

"It's no use getting here just to have our bodies ripped up by those beasts." Marie shuddered.

Peter shook his head. "I read a bit about the park on their website. The lions are in cages."

"You sure?"

"Fairly sure," he said.

"Great," Marie snapped and some of her old fire sparked inside her. "I always wanted to end up as a plate of cat meat."

She tugged at the wire, then felt her way along the fence. By luck, they'd come out within a hundred metres of a gate.

The sighing wind told them there were trees behind the gate. Owls screeched a warning to them to keep out.

"What now?" Marie asked. She stepped closer to Peter and took his hand for comfort and so they wouldn't lose one another in the darkness.

"I think this is where we hand over to Martin and Helen," he said. "We've done what we promised and got them here."

"But even they can't do anything at night," Marie said.

"We can rest," Martin said, suddenly emerging

from hours of quietness. There was a strange excitement in his voice.

"Is that you, Martin?" Marie asked.

"Yes, it's me. Let me speak to Helen," the boy demanded.

"Your manners don't get any better," Marie snapped.

"We are home," Martin said. "This is where we belong. Leave the rest to us."

"If that's all right with Peter," Marie said.

Martin allowed Peter to control the body again. "I suppose he's right," Peter admitted. "The sooner they find what they've come for, the sooner we can get home."

Marie squeezed his hand and said, "See you later, Peter."

Slowly the hands tightened. The girl's back straightened and her chin rose. "Even in the darkness it feels like home," Helen D'Arlay said in her elegant voice.

"Yes," Martin agreed. "We've lived in the darkness for the best part of two hundred years, Helen. It doesn't matter to us. We can sense where we are."

"But we can't walk these bodies through iron gates and stone walls," she reminded him.

"No, but we can climb over them," he said. He tugged her hand and pulled her towards the gates. To the side, there was a wooden door set in the stone wall.

"It's locked."

"But there's a space between the top of the door and the arch above it," Martin said, peering at the gap. The faint glow of the clouded moon revealed the space.

"There are spikes on the top of the door. You've hurt Peter's poor body enough," she reminded him.

"That's why they brought these two bundles of blankets," Martin said. "They must have known they were going to have to climb the railings." He reached up and placed the sleeping bag over the spikes on the top of the door. He placed a foot on the door handle and pulled himself up and over easily.

Martin returned to haul Helen over the top of the door. That was harder. Marie's body was smaller and not as fit as Peter's. By the time she had tumbled onto the gravel behind the door she was exhausted. "We need to rest," she said.

"We're at the west gate now," he said. "If we turn south from here there is shelter where the ground falls away. We can wrap ourselves in these blankets and wait till first light."

He took her hand to lead her into the trees at the side of the drive. She didn't move. "What year is it, Martin?" she said in a whisper barely louder than the wind in the treetops.

"What do you mean?" he asked.

"We've been here before. In 1840. We were running from Inglewilde Hall. My father was chasing us and using the hounds to pick up our scent. We were being hunted like the fox and the deer." Her voice began to rise with the fear and panic of the memory. "We crossed the stream to lose the scent. We sheltered in that hollow and we fell asleep."

"Yes, Helen," he said.

"Maybe we're there now! Maybe we're in 1840 and we'll see my father at the edge of the lake, searching for us."

"No, Helen. He shot me," Martin said. "I died and spent all this time looking for you. I found us two bodies and we've come back to lay my ghost."

"What if that was all a dream?" Helen cried. "What if we fell asleep in 1840 and the shooting, the searching and possessing the bodies was all a dream, Martin? Maybe we've just woken up!"

Chapter Twenty-One

Martin Lane shook his head to clear it. Slowly the wind blew the clouds away from the moon and he stepped away from Helen. He looked at her and smiled a curious smile. "I wish it was a dream, Helen," he said. "But Miss Helen D'Arlay would never, *ever* wear trousers!"

She looked down and felt Marie's denim jeans around her legs. The moonlight glinted on the tears in her eyes. "It was a good dream while it lasted," she murmured.

He gripped her shoulders. "We can't lose,

Helen," he said. "We'll lay my ghost and we'll leave this world together."

"And, if we can't?"

"Then we'll stay. We'll take these bodies and learn to live in this century of theirs," Martin said.

She shook her head. "Peter is strong enough to stop you," she reminded him.

"No! Peter is strong enough to stop me *taking* his body by force. But now he's *given* it to me freely he will never have the strength to take it back from me. And you can do the same to Marie. We'll die together or we'll live together. Either way, we win."

Helen had never wanted it that way. But she knew there was a problem about Martin's plan to lay his ghost. A problem she hadn't been brave enough to tell him yet. A problem that may just stop them from going on to an afterlife together. So another fifty years or so of this life in stolen bodies would be the next best thing. That would mean her stealing Marie's body as Martin would steal Peter's. But she wasn't sure if she could do that. "Let's rest," she said.

He led the way along the old and overgrown paths. Trees had died since their time and new ones had taken their place, but the rising and falling of the land hadn't altered. And Martin knew every rise and hollow of Inglewilde's ancient estate. Even some of the old fox lairs were where they had been in 1840. He could smell the foxes now with the senses of a country boy that even Peter Stone's body couldn't ignore.

At last, where a soft earthen bank shielded them from the wind, they were able to lie down in the sleeping bags and snooze. From time to time, Peter Stone awoke. Each time he did, Martin told him that they were just gathering their strength...that it would all be over in the morning, when Peter could rest easily.

The last time Martin sent Peter back to sleep, he looked up and saw a lightening of the purple-black sky to charcoal grey. He took a firm hold on the body and woke Helen. "Time to go," he said.

"Do you know where you're headed?"

"To the tree by the lake," he said.

"The tree won't be there," she said. "Even the lake may have changed. Do you think you'll still know the place?"

"I'll know it. Like the salmon knows the river it was born in. It's the spot that chains me to this world. I'd find it if I was blindfolded," he said fiercely. He turned and said, "I suppose *you* could find *your* grave. I expect you were buried in the D'Arlay family vaults under a marble tomb?"

"I was not!" she replied angrily. "If you must know I was…"

"What?"

"Nothing," she said quickly.

"Well? How did you die? You never told me."

"You never asked," she said, furiously. "You've been so bitter about the way you died…so busy complaining about how you were murdered by my father…you just can't see how others suffered too. You were not the only person to have suffered a violent death. You weren't the only one condemned to wander the nothingness between this life and the afterlife. Why do you imagine *I* failed to make the journey?"

"I thought you were searching for me," Martin gasped, confused and hurt.

"You *thought* that because it *suited* you to think that. Perhaps yours isn't the *only* ghost that needs to be laid to rest. And, perhaps if you do lay your ghost, you'll go on to the afterlife alone."

"Helen?" he moaned. "How did you die?"

"It doesn't matter now. Let's find your remains."

"I'm not going if you can't come with me! What

would be the point? We'll stay here in these bodies till they die."

"That's theft, Martin. The cruellest sort of theft."

"I'm not leaving without you!" he cried.

She reached up a hand and stroked his cheek. "You may have to. And if you do, it won't be a tragedy. Once you reach the afterlife you'll forget all about me."

"Never...we're together for ever," he told her. *"Till time and times are done."*

"Words, Martin. Just words. If you have to leave without me, then you'll go."

He was left dumb by her words. Before he could say more, she had turned and was striding down a woodland path. She no longer needed him to guide her. She knew exactly where she was going. He began to run after her, sliding down the damp leaves and tripping over branches blown down in autumn gales. When he finally caught her it was because she had stopped.

Helen had halted at the edge of the wood. A lawn sloped down to a reed-choked lake. At the far side of the lake stood an enormous old stone house. Its windows were empty and blind. The morning sun shone through them in places where the roof had collapsed. Shutters and boards hung loosely from the lower windows where someone had tried to protect the ruin from vandals. Small trees grew inside the walls of the house and shattered the glass.

"Inglewilde," she whispered. "What's happened to it?"

"Time has happened to it," Martin said. "What did the preacher say in church? 'How are the mighty fallen?' "

"You see? We can't stay, Martin. We can't live in this world. Not in a world that lets something as lovely as that fall into ruin. We have to leave. Leave it to Peter and Marie. Maybe they can live with this. I can't." Tears ran down her cheeks unchecked.

Martin took her hand, their earlier bitterness forgotten. "How did you die, Helen?" he asked. "You haven't told me yet."

"No, not yet," she said gently.

"How long did you live after your father killed me?"

"Not long."

"Did you die at Inglewilde?"

"Oh, yes."

"Are you buried in the churchyard?"

"No…not the churchyard," she said and she turned her face to him. Though her cheeks were wet with tears, there was a smile on her lips. When they were alive they had understood one another without words. Now he understood everything. Everything.

Chapter Twenty-Two

The lake had changed little. It was oval-shaped, with a tongue of land that reached out almost to the centre.

"The hounds picked up our scent on the edge of the woods there," Martin said. He was calm now that he understood. "It was a mistake for us to run down the hill and back towards the house."

"You thought we could run through the water at the edge of the lake and make them lose the scent again," Helen said kindly.

"But by then they'd seen us." Martin shrugged.

"Once they had sight of us the scent didn't matter."

"No one can outrun hounds. Not even a stag."

They stepped onto the spit of land that ran into the lake. It was overgrown with tall reeds arching across on either side. No one would have guessed there was solid earth underneath. "We ran out to the end of this strip of land. It was clearer then." They pushed reeds out of the way and disturbed frogs that leaped into the water with dull splashes. "It's a dead end, of course," Martin said. "There was nowhere left for us to run."

"But there was," Helen said. "There was the tree. A beautiful old oak tree. We'd take picnics out from the hall and sit under the shade of that tree. With the lake on three sides it was almost like being on an island."

"There was the tree," Martin admitted. It was colder now, here on this damp earth with rotting weeds under their feet. There was no heat in the rising sun.

"That was your plan, Martin," Helen reminded him. "You would run into this dead end and let the hounds catch you. But you would lift me up into that great tree. Even in the autumn there were enough leaves for me to hide until it was safe to come down."

"I suppose so," the boy admitted. "I suppose it was a sort of plan."

"You knew they'd catch you. Punish you. But you risked that to save me. That was noble of you."

"It's not just the folk with noble blood, like the D'Arlays, that can act noble," he said stiffly.

"I know, Martin." Helen smiled.

"And I didn't expect to die. I knew I could manage the hounds. They were mad with the hunt and they wanted blood. But I'd worked with the dogs as well as with the horses. Those hounds knew my voice. They were baying and snarling, but once they heard my voice they backed off."

"I know," Helen reminded him. "I was in the tree."

"Then your father came down out of the woods and he was as blood-hungry as his hounds...worse. He demanded to know what I'd done with his daughter. I told him I'd set you on a horse outside the gates and that you were riding to meet me at a secret place he'd never find."

"I heard you."

"But you didn't see him. The veins in his neck were swollen purple and close to bursting. His eyes were blood-red and bulging. He was screaming at me to tell him where you were. He said he'd count to three. If I didn't tell him then he'd shoot me. I was calm, Helen. So calm. I laughed at him and said that if he shot me he'd *never* find you. I think it was my laugh that finally drove him to do it. I didn't even hear the shot. Just felt something like a punch in the chest, then a red shutter closing over my eyes. No pain."

"You were brave," Helen D'Arlay said.

The boy shrugged. "It was a waste. I meant to save us. But I didn't. I failed."

The girl kneeled on a small mound of earth at the edge of the lake. It was all that was left of the old oak.

"You saved me," she said.

"For how long? Why won't you tell me?"

"For a few minutes," she said softly.

"The hounds killed you? My plan failed?" the boy moaned.

"It was my fault," she said. "When I heard the shot I screamed. I let myself slide down through the branches and crashed down in front of my father. If I'd stayed silent, then your plan would have worked. I picked up your head and looked into your eyes. Wide eyes, surprised, but lifeless. That's when I threatened him."

"You threatened Lord D'Arlay?"

"I told him that what he'd done was murder. That I'd go to the law officers and I'd see him hang. He pulled out his other pistol and pointed it at me. Told me to be quiet. Told me he'd shoot me as easily as he'd shot you. All that mattered to him were his sons. A daughter was nothing. He only tried to stop us running away together because of the disgrace it would bring to the D'Arlay name. He wasn't bothered about *me*."

"But to shoot his own daughter," Martin groaned. "How could he?"

"Because I *told* him to. If you were dead, then I wanted to join you. I told him I would never give him any peace. I'd hound him till the day he died…or the day I died."

"But he shot me in anger," the boy said, shaking his head. "How could he shoot you in cold blood?"

"He was mad, Martin, *mad*. And he panicked when he saw his daughter screaming at him and threatening him. He squeezed the trigger to silence me. I fell beside you, just here." As the boy kneeled beside her, she smiled. "That's the way I'd have wanted it."

"And afterwards?"

"I felt a lightness, as if I were drifting up towards the clouds. I could look down and see us lying there below. I tried to hold on. To stay, but everything was fading and I was too far away to reach it."

"So you don't know what he did with our bodies?"

She closed her eyes and placed her hands flat on the soft earth. "I saw my father scrabbling here at the soil. I think he planned to bury you where you fell. Your body is here, Martin. Here under our feet."

"And yours?"

She shook her head. "That's what I don't know, Martin. I may be here with you. I hope so."

"And if you're not?"

"Then I can't join you in the afterlife. You have to go on alone."

Chapter Twenty-Three

The earth was damp but sandy and easy to scrape away. Lord D'Arlay had not buried the bodies very deep. He'd had little time and relied on the fact that no one was looking for Martin Lane under the ground. He encouraged the rumour that the boy had abducted his daughter and probably taken her to London where no one would ever find them.

Helen and Martin worked silently and carefully with a fear of what they'd find. After a few minutes of working Helen looped her finger around a strip of leather and tugged at it. Fastened onto the leather was a miniature horse. "It's the necklace you carved for me out of a piece of bone," she said.

As she stroked the ornament, she felt a shudder like an electric shock and a giddiness.

"Oh, Martin – it's me! It's enough to set me free!" she gasped.

"But what about me?" the boy demanded. "We have to find *me*!"

Helen swayed and closed her eyes. For a few moments she seemed to slip from the body of Marie Allen and look down on the scene as she had so many years before.

"Helen!" Martin cried. "Not yet! Not again! Wait."

Helen forced herself to pour back into the borrowed body and dropped the horse necklace. "Hurry, Martin. I can't seem to hold on much longer."

"You have to! We've come too far for one of us to leave without the other!"

The boy scraped furiously at the shallow trench while the girl helped him. Martin gave a cry. A silver chain caught in his fingers and he pulled up a locket. It was blackened with age but he rubbed it hard against his jacket and made out the engraving. He traced it with his finger. It was a single letter. "It was the first letter you taught me," he said. "That's an 'aitch' and it stands for Helen!" Martin pushed a thumbnail into the edge of the silver casing and forced it open. Inside was a tiny enamel portrait of Helen D'Arlay. He showed it to the girl and they smiled. "Your gift to me," he said.

They picked up their ancient mementoes and stood up. Martin smoothed some of the soft soil back into the hollows and said, "Let the rest stay there. We have all we need."

They walked back to the shore of the lake and passed the shattered walls of the old house. They climbed over the matted grass and brambles at the side. It seemed as if their feet were scarcely touching the ground or even leaving footprints in the dew.

A studded door in a tall, moss-crusted wall led into a neglected graveyard. The headstones fell drunkenly in all directions. Yellow lichen and silver snail tracks hid the rain-worn words of the forgotten dead. Martin wanted Helen to read the inscriptions. "Find out what happened to the people we knew."

She kept walking towards the corner where an ancient yew tree grew. "It doesn't matter, Martin. Not any more. They've all gone."

He paused for a moment and looked around, almost scenting the air with his nostrils. "You're right, Helen. There are no ghosts in graveyards. They've all been laid to rest properly. They've no need to stay the way we did."

They moved on and stopped under the dripping branches of the yew. "Here," she said simply. "We'll rest here."

Martin took the horse pendant and the locket. He used a sharp stone to scoop a hollow between the massive roots. "What are the words?" he asked. "Something about ashes to ashes and dust to dust?"

"We don't need words." Helen grinned. "We don't need headstones or prayers or coffins or mourners. We just need to be in our rightful place, together."

He took her hand. There was a sighing wind in the old tree. The air seemed to twist and suck at dead leaves and send them rattling against the grey headstones. The early morning cloud parted again and let a ray of sunshine into the walled graveyard. As light shone along that narrow beam, something travelled outwards and upwards.

The dawn sun lit the faces of two young people who stood with hands joined.

The boy looked embarrassed and the girl confused.

"Peter?" she asked. "Is that you, Peter?"

"Yes," the boy said slowly. "Yes, Martin's gone. Gone completely. And Helen?"

"It's as if she'd never been here," the girl said.

"The haunting's finished, then?" he asked.

"Yeah. And our problems have only just begun," she told him.

Chapter Twenty-Four

Mr. Stone sat next to the head teacher. His weather-beaten face was grey. The Head was pouring tea. "You shouldn't have come in this morning. We could cover."

The teacher cleared his throat, awkwardly. "I couldn't think of anywhere else to go."

"We've told the police that Peter's missing and that he's probably with Marie Allen. They'll do their best. They'll find them."

"And then what?"

"Then they'll bring him home."

"And he'll leave as soon as he's old enough. I can't blame him. I've been too hard on the lad."

"You're too hard on your*self*," the Head said quietly.

Mr. Stone thought about it for a long time. "He's got a right to make his own life with his own friends. I…I didn't know I'd miss him so much when he left. When I found he was gone this morning, well…"

"Marie Allen isn't a bad girl. She's a strong character and she stands up for herself," the Head explained. "That's exactly what you wanted from Peter, isn't it?"

"Yes."

"Then perhaps some of her strength will rub off onto him. Give them a chance."

The telephone rang and the Head snatched it from its cradle. "I said I wasn't to be disturbed…oh, I see…yes. Thank you."

He turned to Mr. Stone. "It seems a boy and a girl were seen boarding a train for London last night. They got off at Northallerton. The local police are on their way there now. They'll be all right."

The pupils milled around in groups, waiting for the doors to open and allow them to surge into the warmth. Only one boy stood alone and out of the huddles of friends. He wore a leather jacket and his podgy face was turning purple under one eye. He pushed himself off the wall and walked over to a group of boys. "Hi, lads!" The boys looked at one another and exchanged secret smirks. "I see Stoney hasn't come in this morning. Guess he's scared of me, huh?"

"Thought you might be scared of him," one of the boys sniggered.

Andy King scowled. "Stone could never be that lucky again. If I hadn't slipped…"

A bell rang and the gang walked towards the glass doors, laughing. The boy in the leather jacket called after them. "I did! You saw it! I slipped. I'd have murdered him otherwise!"

The laughter echoed down the bare corridors of the school.

When the bank doors opened, the old man was first to enter.

"Good morning, Doctor Black," the counter assistant smiled brightly. "What can we do for you today?"

"I'd like to see the manager, please, the hypnotist said. In the harsh light of the morning he looked frail and tired. He clutched at the morning newspaper. The faces of Peter and Marie looked out at him from under the headline: *Teenagers missing*.

"Have you an appointment?"

"No, no. It's something that's just come up. Something I decided this morning – I need to talk to the manager as soon as possible."

The assistant nodded. "I'm sure he wouldn't want to keep a doctor waiting," she said.

"Doctor? A title, my dear. A title I used for my stage act. 'The Mysterious Doctor Black' sounded better than 'Herbert the Hypnotist Black'," he said awkwardly.

"Sounds fascinating."

"It was…but I'm getting too old for that sort of thing now. Too old. Too…careless. I've woken too many sleeping secrets that should be left hidden."

The woman picked up a telephone and punched in a number. "I'll see if the manager can see you. Can I tell her what it is in connection with?"

"With my pension scheme," the old man said. "I want to talk about the arrangements for my retirement. You see…I was going to write a book that would make my fortune. But now…I'm afraid that it'll never be written. I just can't do it any more…"

"Where are we?" Peter asked. He knew he was cold, hungry, tired and lost. Yet he felt content. Like an exhausted traveller who's reached the end of a journey and finally laid down his load.

"Somewhere near Northallerton," Marie said. She too seemed satisfied.

"We're in a graveyard," the boy said. He looked at his stained hands and then at the soil. "We've just buried something there," he said.

"Leave it," Marie warned him. "It's probably better if we don't know."

He nodded and began to walk towards the door set in the wall. They walked around the ruined house and looked over a stagnant, overgrown lake. A weed-choked drive led through a tunnel of trees to fine iron gates.

"It must have been a magnificent place once," Marie said.

"It's not the stones that make a great house. It's the people," he said.

"It was a home to Helen and Martin," she said. "I can't imagine a place like this being home."

Marie looked down the drive. A white car was now parked there. A man and a woman in navy uniforms stood watching the boy and girl.

"Trouble," she said.

Peter shrugged. He turned and took one last look at the lake. "There are worse things."

"Worse than facing a father like yours?" she joked. "What's worse than that?"

They walked on towards the waiting car. "Haunting yourself," he said. "Haunting yourself."

MORE CHILLING STORIES TO KEEP YOU AWAKE AT NIGHT...

Usborne Thrillers

SANDRA GLOVER

Demon's Rock

There's something evil
out there...

ISBN: 0 7460 6037 8

MALCOLM ROSE

The Tortured Wood

Who will be the next
victim?

ISBN: 0 7460 6035 1

ANN EVANS

The Beast

How can you kill
something that's
already dead?

ISBN: 0 7460 6034 3

PAUL STEWART

The Curse of Magoria

Will anyone escape the
deadly dance of time?

ISBN: 0 7460 6232 X

All books are priced at £4.99